La Luce's Legacy

Inheritance of Seduction, Secrets, and Scandal

Dirk Mourningwood

Melisa,
Matteo wouldn't have gotten to his story if not for you.
Thank you for pushing me forward.

Also By Dirk

Other works by Dirk Mourningwood
La Luce's Legacy (2024)
Eros Unzipped (2024)
Eros Unchained (2024)

From Dirk

La Luce's Legacy began as a serialized story on Kindle Vella with a new chapter coming out twice a month. But who even knows that exists? Pretty soon, my regular readers were pleading for a novel, and I'm nothing if not accommodating.

Have fun in the sun, but don't forget your protection.

<u>Trigger warnings</u> include but are not limited to voyeurism, sexual intercourse without protection or discussion about safe sex, scenes that may contain questionable consent before or during sexual acts, rough sex, and, of course, strong language and graphic sex acts.

One

Paradise

T HEY SAY MONEY CAN'T buy happiness, but in our society, it sure can buy an approximation close enough for me.

My father passed away on my fortieth birthday. I found out almost a year later when a lawyer knocked on my apartment door, carrying a briefcase of paperwork for me to sign. A week later, I was flying first class to a Mediterranean island I'd never heard of to see an ocean-front resort. Apparently, my old man owned it, so now I did.

After a layover in Amsterdam and another in Rome, we landed on Isola di Luce in the late afternoon, where it was forty degrees warmer than when I got on the first flight in Minnesota. I'd gladly get used to this temperature. For now, I patted a handkerchief to my neck as the lawyer, Mister Marco Andretti, drove us through the winding, narrow streets to the resort. His little convertible sports car tore through an old but impeccably tended quaint village, the tires rumbling on the cobblestone as we passed colorful shops, cafes, and dozens of hot, dark-haired, olive-skinned men. It seemed completely implausible that the entire town would be populated with attractive gentlemen, yet that's all I saw.

"Your father acquired Isola di Luce twenty years ago and worked tirelessly since to restore it and build the resort," Mister Andretti said, often taking his eyes from the sharp turns in the road. My hands gripped my knees until my knuckles were white. "His goal was to make it the Mediterranean's premier, exclusive vacation and recreation destination. He was nearly there before his illness caught up with him." Andretti choked up. The man had been dead a year but clearly meant something here. I hadn't seen my old man in over thirty years, and now his death resulted in two commas in my bank account, a trip to a luxury island, and zero tears shed.

The island was only a bit more than eight miles end to end—thirteen kilometers, that is. I'd have to get used to metric. I expected an island smaller than my little hometown to be completely filled, end to end, but once we were outside of the city, more of a village, with the airport, there was nothing but terraced hillsides and rows of olive trees.

Andretti slowed at a heavy gate with a guard post beside it. The watchman came out immediately, dressed in a tight pink polo and blue shorts, holding a clipboard.

"Mister Andretti, sir. Everyone will be happy to see you home." The guard's grin widened when he looked at me. "You must be Mister Matteo Demetri-ou. I'm honored to welcome you to La Luce. I am so sorry for your loss. Your father was a great man."

The man's accent made everything sound a little sexier, even my name.

"Thank you, Vezio," said the lawyer.

The guard nodded, reached into his booth, and the gate silently slid to the side. I nodded to Vezio as we passed him. The road hung close to hug high cliffs to the crashing waves below, with an olive grove neatly arranged on the other side.

"Freshwater was an early concern," said Andretti. "Your father solved that with a genius desalination plant on the island's north side. That plant and a few solar and wind farms provide ample electricity. Olives and olive oil are Isola di Luce's official exports and business, along with some luxury goods, such as the wares tailored by Herr Benedikt Jensen, who you will soon meet."

I expected La Luce to be like the town we'd passed through, a well-maintained but quite old, cobbled-together mash of buildings.

We rounded the last corner through the grove, and I finally saw it.

La Luce rose from the ruins of generations past, dozens of buildings knitted together by narrow stone streets or boardwalk paths. The main build-ing was itself a marvel of modern architecture. The four-story structure was open on the first level to-ward the sea. The second and third levels might have had restaurants or spas behind the curved glass. A balcony ran from the second level out to a transparent pool that flowed out and down into the crystal clear lagoon dotted with sand bars, smooth rocky outcroppings, and bright yellow chaises. Beyond, a white sugar sand beach separated the lagoon from the gently lapping Mediterranean Sea. As we drove closer to the central building, I made out the private cabins along the beach connected to a main boardwalk and those I assumed to be staff at work in pink shirts and blue shorts.

Paradise.

"This looks done to me," I said when we pulled into the spot closest to the front entrance. "What could be left to do before opening?"

"Work has continued since your father's passing, but the paperwork requires his, now your, signature and signoff. We are currently undergoing a soft launch, as the phrase goes. We are working out the last kinks in our supply chains and letting the few guests in the resort test the amenities." He nodded to two men laid out on the yellow chaises. "Then we will contact our curated client list for the grand opening in two weeks."

"Curated list?" It made sense for a high-end resort to be invite-only, but I hadn't thought about how those invites would be chosen.

Andretti pulled his briefcase from the back seat, set it on his lap, and walked his fingers through it, pulling out a single sheet. I didn't recognize any of the names but noticed they had one thing in common: They were all men.

"What did you mean by exclusive?" I asked.

"La Luce is to be an all-inclusive, intensely private, all-male resort."

"A gay resort?"

Andretti frowned. "Your father never liked such confining language. Bi, pan, trans. All men would be welcome here. Sexuality does not matter."

"Was my father gay?"

"Again, he never liked such titles. I worked with him for twenty years and never saw him with a woman."

"He was with my mother."

The lawyer hummed, tucking the client sheet away and pushing open the car door. "That hardly means anything."

Maybe I had more in common with my old man than I knew.

"What do we need to do to plan this grand opening?" I asked, watching a tanned and muscled gardener wipe the sweat from his brow. He nodded when he noticed my attention, touching a gloved hand to the brim of his wide straw hat.

"That can be a matter for tomorrow," said the lawyer.

I paused in front of a giant, silent fan blowing a cool mist, letting it puff out my shirt. At home, I'd had the heat on for a month. At least it would get cooler through the winter, giving me a chance to acclimate. No weather app had Isola di Luce, but Malta was close enough, and I assumed the weather would be about the same. I inhaled the cool, misty air deeply, letting it chill me to my spine.

I stepped into the main lobby, filled with potted palm trees and a huge window looking out on
the pool in the center. Everything was immaculate,
gleaming in the afternoon sun, tended by staff in
their uniforms of pink linen shirts and light blue
shorts.

Andretti was walking back from the reception
desk, offering me a key. "It's been a long trip. We can
discuss legal matters and the opening after dinner.
Why don't you retire to your suite? Settle in. Take
off your shoes. Relax for a moment."

I owned this place. Of course I'd have a suite.
"Where is it?" I ran a thumb down the brass key's
smooth blade, clearly a stylized electronic keycard.

Andretti nodded to the elevator nestled between
plush leather benches. "Penthouse. I'll send someone up with a change of clothes. Set an alarm if
you lie down. We have dinner with the managers
tonight at seven and a major meeting with the core
investors the day after tomorrow. Spend the time
familiarizing yourself with the resort and amenities.
Relax, get to know the staff and guests."

I thanked him and stepped into the elevator that
looked pulled from a timeless art deco hotel. After
sliding the key into the slot beside the oblong button labeled "Penthouse," the door sighed closed and,
a moment later, opened to a breathtaking view of
the Mediterranean Sea sparkling beyond the wall of
floor-to-ceiling windows.

Light streamed into the suite from skylights, shin-
ing on the potted ferns and palm trees carefully and
intentionally placed around the room. A television

wider than my arm span sat in a pit in front of seating for six. More if you're cozy. The dining table might have been made of driftwood from the beach, but it looked higher class than anything I'd eaten off of. The kitchen was fully stocked with an even mix of ready-made microwave meals and dry goods to cook something more substantial. Nothing fresh, though.

Following a mirrored hallway, I found the bathroom, a masterpiece of granite and nickel that wasn't much less square footage than my entire apartment a week ago. A claw-foot tub dominated the center, with an open shower to one side and a double sink to the other. The toilet was tucked away around the corner. Back in the main room, behind a floral screen separating it from the entertainment area, I found the huge circular bed with bedding that matched the beach below. Standing at the foot of the bed, I looked out over the resort. It felt like a vacation. One that I could never afford before.

This was paradise, and I'd given up everything to be here. Not that I'd had much. A closet and dresser full of clothes that no longer fit after I'd started going to the gym again. Chipped dishware from my Nana and a TV with a slowly spreading corner of dead pixels. A dead-end job and a tiny apartment. I could have afforded better if not for my most recent ex, Pete, dragging me down and backward for years. Maybe that's what would make La Luce perfect, the fact that Pete would never come scratching at the door at midnight, reeking of Old Milwaukee and cigarettes and offering me a handjob if I let him stay the night "just one more time."

The elevator chimed as I finished a cursory exploration of the two-thousand-square-foot apartment, and a screen beside the elevator lit up, showing a man in his early twenties waiting in the elevator car. Wearing the now-familiar uniform of short blue trunks and a pink collared shirt stretched over his broad shoulders, he raised the garment bag draped over his left arm and smiled up at the camera.

I smashed the green "ACCEPT" button on the screen.

A few seconds later, the doors opened. He was so much more impressive in person, with how he stressed the seams of his shirt around his arms and across his chest. "I have clothing for you, Mister Demetriou." His deep voice was heavily accented, spoken around a strong jaw sporting a day's stubble.

"You can call me Matteo," I said, stepping close to take the bag from him. It took my every effort not to get even closer, to breathe in the scent he wore, something woody and musky.

His gray eyes bore into me. "Can I do anything else for you while I am here, Mister Matteo?" He grinned.

"Just Matteo, no mister." I laid the garment bag across the back of a chair by the windows. "Thank you for the clothes, but I should be fine now. I thought I'd take a hot bath and wash off my travels."

"Let me draw it for you."

I opened my mouth to object. I could run my own bath, but he was already halfway down the mirrored hall. The water started behind me while I took a moment to inspect the clothing he'd brought. Loose, cream-colored linen pants and a white shirt with a deep V. Nothing had a tag, but they looked my size. Standing at the window, looking out to the sea, I wondered how long it would take to set in that this was now my resort. I lived here. I owned this. I had property, a business, and employees. Very soon, the wealthy recluses of the world would come to me. Some were already here for this soft launch. I didn't recognize the names on Andretti's client sheet, but now I imagined they were all pseudonyms for senators and world-class rugby players. Stock market billionaires and oil barons. Andretti mentioned meeting with investors, and those men had to be loaded to pay for part of this extravagance. They would expect nothing short of perfection when they arrived.

Rose oil and sandalwood overwhelmed me before I stepped into the bathroom. The assistant...? Shit.

"I'm sorry, I didn't ask your name."

"Lio."

Lio sat on the edge of the porcelain tub, dragging his fingers through the rising water. In the building heat from the bath, he'd undone the top two buttons of his pink shirt, showing a small silver ankh on a chain nestled in his chest hair.

"Have you considered who you might hire as your personal valet?" After watching a lot of British television, it sounded odd to hear "valet" pronounced correctly. Though, everything sounded a touch sexier in Lio's voice.

"Will I need one?" I grinned, standing awkwardly at the door.

"You will. Operating La Luce will be strenuous, Mister Matteo. You will want someone to see to your... personal care. Please," he turned off the water and gestured to the tub. He raised a large sponge loofa in the other hand, gripping it to squeeze water down his thick, hairy forearms. "Let me wash your back."

If this was all part of his interview, I didn't know if I needed to see other candidates vying for the position. Pulling off my shirt, I crossed to the tub, catching the scent of his cologne, even over the oils in the bath water. Stepping out of my shoes and unbuckling my belt, Lio's gray eyes burned into me. What was I doing? I wasn't the type of guy to strip and let a complete stranger bathe me. I wasn't a millionaire two weeks ago, either. My anxiety melted away with the heat and steam. His tongue licked across his upper lip when I let my shorts and trunks drop. It had been too long since I'd been naked in front of a stranger, and never one as hot as Lio.

One hand instinctively cupped my balls and half-chubbed cock as I stepped into the water on the verge of being too hot.

"Are you quite comfortable, Mister Matteo?" His fingers still dragged through the water, inches from my thighs.

I wasn't hating the "Mister" anymore and didn't correct him. "It's perfect, Lio. Thank you."

He billowed air into his shirt with his dry hand. "It is quite warm. Might I take off my shirt?" He popped one button and was fingering the next.

"Shirt, shorts, whatever makes you comfortable." I sank deeper until the water covered my shoulders, biting my tongue from inviting him to join me. A decade in corporate America and HR videos flashed in my mind.

No, fuck it. This was my resort, my island. My private island. I wasn't even in a country. I'd invite an employee to sit on my cock if I wanted. No, a consenting adult who happens to be in my employ.

Lio chuckled, letting the pink linen slide from his sculpted shoulders. My eyes ran over his dark nipples obscured behind thick chest hair that I longed to touch. A bright blue tattoo of a fish peeked from around his ribs, and another of what might be tribal markings around his left bicep. He stretched his neck, showing the cords of muscle down the side.

Lifting the spongey loofa from where it floated, he squeezed the water out slowly. An array of soaps were stacked across the side of the tub, and he picked one without pausing. Thick body wash the color of honey oozed from the bottle, flowing over the sponge and his fingers. Squeezing again, white foam pressed through his hand to float across the water's surface.

"Lean forward," he whispered, moving around to squat behind me. I did, sitting up so the water was around my lower ribs. The soft loofa wiped across my shoulders, easing away the tension of a day's travel.

"That's perfect," I said, almost moaning, folding forward to expose my back fully to him, my forehead coming near to the water's rippling surface.

He dropped the loofa, gripping my shoulders with powerful hands, prying at the kinks and knots, working down to my shoulder blades, rubbing a knuckle along the muscle beside my spine. Lower, dipping his hands into the water to push at my lower back. Even with what limited angle he must have had, it felt amazing, melting my tension away.

"Tell me something about yourself, Lio. Did you grow up on the island?"

He chuckled, and I felt him move closer. His breath tickled my neck. "No, Mister Matteo. I moved to Isola di Luce two years ago when I was twenty."

"You're a lot of man for twenty-two." I reached over my head to guide his hands to my chest so I could lean back, tilting my head to look up into his gray eyes. "That's much better, Lio. Thank you." My hands were still over his wrists, his palms flat against my ribs. He slid his pinky and ring fingers against me, caressing me.

"What else can I do for you, Mister Matteo?" He moved closer, chest hair brushing my shoulders as his right hand slipped lower under the water across my belly. Despite the water's leeching heat, I couldn't have been harder, bobbing against the back of Lio's wrist.

"I shouldn't stay in here all day." I shifted my hips, rubbing my dick against his wrist. "Andretti has a lot of paperwork for me to look over. I have to prepare to meet the investors. I can finish up myself."

"Mister Andretti does not like to be kept waiting." Lio flattened his hand on my belly, sliding down, curling his fingers around my thigh, and catching the base of my cock with his thumb. His lips touched my ear. "But Mister Andretti is not the boss, Mister Matteo. You do as you wish. All on Isola di Luce serve at your pleasure." His hand tightened around my girth as he licked my ear, nuzzling against it with his nose. His warm breath sent a shiver down my spine. "But be careful. Not all on the island wish for your success, not as I do." He gave my dick one more squeeze, then let his fingers trail from it and out of the water.

I pivoted toward him, feeling my shoulders reknit, undoing Lio's work as I sat naked in the tub before a stranger. "That sounds ominous, Lio."

He fingered the ankh hanging on his chest. "I should not say more."

"I very much think you should." I gestured for him to hand me a towel.

He looked away with a sharp breath, then turned back to me, licking his lips. "Some would like the island returned to how it was before your father took over, and some whisper of being upset that La Luce was signed over to you, to one who never knew it existed."

"I imagine those two groups would overlap." I wrapped the soft cotton around my waist and ran my hands over my arms and chest. My skin had never felt so soft after the oils and lotions of the bath. "What do you mean by returning the island to how it was? Closing the resort?"

Lio picked at his fingers nervously. "I wouldn't know, Mister Matteo. It's only rumors." Despite his clear anxiety, he looked amazing in his little blue shorts, powerful back and arm muscles casting sharp shadows as he bent to pick up his pink linen shirt.

"Rumors and whispers have a funny way of turning into actions. Why are you telling me this, Lio?"

He bit his lower lip and shook his head once. "Forget I said anything. It's nothing."

I absolutely couldn't just forget it, not with how Lio avoided eye contact and didn't crack a dismissive grin. He knew a lot more than he was saying, but this method of questioning wasn't working. "You want me to succeed here. What does that look like for you?"

He glanced up with a softened expression. "I want La Luce to thrive."

"I didn't know about it until a few days ago, and you're fine with me running it?"

He shrugged, then nodded. "Honestly, it makes no difference to me. If you share even a drop of your father's passion, it will be more than we need."

Did I share his passion? What was his passion? I knew nothing about the man I was to replace. "If I commit to that, will you help me, Lio? I'll do everything I can for La Luce and what's right for the island."

He stepped close, running a finger down my forearm. "What if you can't do both?"

"I'll have to decide then." I stepped from the tub, running my hand across his solid chest as I passed him on my way back to the main room. I touched the window's curved glass and surveyed the sprawling resort and sea beyond. "Do you think anyone means me harm?" Staff in pink and blue moved below, seeing to whatever tasks kept them busy. "If people are upset about La Luce for one reason or another, they'd be upset with me."

Lio moved beside me, his shoulder brushing mine. He rolled his neck and tapped a finger on the glass. "Yes. Some wished your father harm, so those feelings may have transferred to you."

I'd never asked Andretti how my father died; he just mentioned my father being sick, and I left it at that. I suppose it didn't matter to me before that moment. Lio's wording implied there was something intentional in what led to me owning La Luce. My face flushed as my head swam with plots. The village I landed in an hour ago was old. As were the bits of ruins built into the structure of La Luce's spas and restaurants. Did my father push the natives off? They wanted their island back and wanted the resort to fail, so they killed my old man? Or maybe someone from within the staff hoped to disrupt the ownership and take control? Who would own La Luce if something were to happen to me? Perhaps something with one of the investors?

Suddenly, everyone was a suspect. Every gorgeous man in that little village I'd arrived in wanted his island back. Every gardener and front desk attendant wanted his share of what the resort attracted. There was no reason to trust Lio, but I had to trust someone. I needed someone to anchor me in these seas I'd fallen into, a liferaft.

"Would you help me, Lio? Guide me?"

He turned toward me, leaning against the glass, hooking a thumb into the belt loop of his tight blue shorts. His pink shirt hung from his other hand. "Yes. I'll be your lighthouse, Mister Matteo. Your beacon in the dark."

I cupped a palm to his cheek, tracing my fingertips through his rough stubble. "Thank you, Lio." My hand slipped to his chest, to his silver ankh, the Egyptian symbol for life. "I should get down to Andretti." Goddammit. Even with thoughts of corporate or political espionage, my balls ached from being teased and left without release.

His hand shot to mine as I pulled away, his gray gaze burning into me. He squeezed, then reached both hands to unclasp his necklace. It hung from his fist, catching the sun beaming through the window before he reached behind me, fastening it around my neck. "For luck." Keeping a hand on either side of my face, he kissed my left cheek, then my right. "For La Luce." He pressed his lips to mine for just a breath, then backed away, walking toward the elevator.

I don't know how long I stood there, eyes unfocused, a finger tracing my lips.

My phone rang, knocking me from my stupor, and I noticed my two suitcases and bags at the foot of the bed. Someone must have delivered those while Lio bathed me. I rushed to it, digging through for my purse and cell phone.

"Hello?"

"Mister Demetriou, I hope you are settling in well," said a familiar voice.

"Yes, Mister Andretti. I was just getting dressed."

"Excellent. I don't mean to rush you, but I must brief you on a matter before dinner. I will see you shortly." He hung up without a farewell.

Standing beside the bed, wearing just a towel, I flipped through my notifications, dismissing a dozen from social media and games. The last was a message in ChatSphere, an app I hadn't used in almost a decade. The number was twelve digits long, completely foreign to my American senses. The message itself made my heart skip a beat.

> +34 58 4115 7011: Your father was murdered. Trust no one.

Two
Balcony

I STARED AT THE message until the phone slipped from my numb fingers.

> +34 58 4115 7011: Your father was murdered. Trust no one.

It blasted any thoughts of meeting with Andretti, the managers, or the investors from my mind. A mark might be on my head now if the message was true. No, there were plenty of reasons to commit homicide outside of wanting to take control of a resort. Maybe it was a jilted lover in a moment of passion or any number of other things besides owning La Luce. I couldn't let myself devolve into paranoia without knowing more. I at least had to find out about my father, specifically the circumstances around his death. Picking up my phone from where I'd dropped it on my bags, another point hit me. Someone had delivered my luggage while I was in the bath with Lio. If someone meant me harm, they were only an elevator ride away. It took a key to get to the penthouse, but how many copies of that were floating around?

"Stop this, Matteo," I tried to psych myself up but could hear the anxiety in my voice.

Throwing the towel across the bed, I walked naked to where I'd left the garment bag Lio brought. Pausing under one of the skylights, I raised my face to the warm sun, stretching my shoulders back with a deep breath. Fuck, if someone wanted me out of the way, at least I'd get a few days in this paradise. The balcony beyond the curved glass windows called to me, and I longed to go out there, to stretch out nude in the full sun. Having lived in Minnesota most of my life, I never had such a chance before. The clothes slung over the chair, and Andretti's impatient call nagged at me, but they could wait a few more minutes.

As Lio said, all on Isola di Luce serve at my pleasure.

A clever, nearly invisible door opened to the balcony, and I stepped from the thick shag of the suite to the wide composite wood planks. The sun crashed over me, warming me to the bones with a tickle across my back, telling me I'd be sweating before long out here. I crossed to the railing, gripped the curved, polished wood, closed my eyes, and took another deep breath. Exhaling toward the Mediterranean, I let my gaze drift over the resort below. I'd seen a few maps over the last couple of days, but not enough to identify all the buildings. A pale boardwalk made of the same material as the balcony connected spas, private baths, restaurants, exercise centers, a rental hall, and a theatre. Two stories down, one of the many pools was directly under the balcony. Employees in pink and blue continued their work, none pausing to look up at me standing with my dick out. A man who I assumed to be one of the soft launch guests was just gathering up his things to exit the pool area.

The thought pulsed a bit of blood, and my balls reminded me of the ache left by Lio. A memory returned of how I shifted my hips to rub my dick against his wrist, how he'd gripped me with a single squeeze. My hand slipped around my thigh as he had, wrapping my thumb around the base and cupping my balls in my fingers. Now I was fully hard, a rock in my hand, and this time, it wouldn't be ignored. With my left elbow on the railing, the sun basked across my back. Gripping my dick, smooth as ever from the bath oils, with images of the ankh dangling in Lio's chest hair, I barely got ten strokes in before I felt the climax rushing forward, weakening my knees. There was no stopping it. Thick blasts of cum shot onto the glass under the railing's wood top. Staggering back on quaking legs, I chuckled at my mess, watching it slide to the composite wood flooring.

"I think someone's out to murder me, so I jerk off on the balcony."

A few minutes in the sun with a fresh, salty sea breeze and I'd become a completely different man.

When Marco Andretti knocked on my apartment door last week, it didn't take long for me to list what I'd give up leaving Bloomington, Minnesota. It was a very short list. I had no family in the area after my father left, and my mother suddenly moved us from New York thirty years ago. I had a few friends, mostly through work, but none for whom I'd give up this opportunity. My job was fine enough: working at a data strategy firm, plugging numbers into spreadsheets all day, and looking for trends. I loathed the idea of "putting myself back out there" and starting fresh on a relationship I knew wouldn't last. They never did. If I had even a houseplant to miss me, I might not have followed Andretti to the airport. But much like relationships, I killed every one of those. The lawyer said he'd take care of whatever was left in my apartment, but I wasn't sure what he'd done with my car. Sold it for scrap, I didn't care.

Holding my dick to keep from dripping on the carpet, I jogged inside for a paper towel from the kitchen. That smeared my work rather than cleaned it, but at least it picked up enough to stop it from running more. I'd have to clean it properly after dinner. As I stood from my squat, I gave the resort one more look and noticed a single employee in uniform staring up at me. He stood beside a neatly trimmed hedge at the far side of the pool. At this distance, I couldn't make out many of his details other than that he was clean-shaven under a straw hat, a gardener. A breath later, he disappeared behind the hedge.

Had he been there the whole time?

My phone rang inside and I rushed for it, fumbling for where I'd thrown it in with my luggage. I recognized Andretti's number.

"Yes, hello. I'm on my way," I said as a greeting.

"Thank you, Mister Demetriou." He hung up.

I dressed quickly, not quite able to shake the last vestiges of my corporate indoctrination.

Three

Old Fashioned

"I WAS READY TO call for a search party." Andretti sat behind a round table shrouded in ivory linen, one of the dozen spread across the restaurant dangling over a cliff to the Mediterranean Sea below. The lawyer swirled a glass of red wine in one hand; the other rested beside a leather briefcase on the table. He'd showered and changed since our arrival, now wearing a white shirt with soft pinstripes and dark gray linen slacks. The delicate platinum chain hanging just below his collarbone matched the watch on his wrist. I would have assumed he was somewhere in his sixties, having worked for my father as long as he had, and by the deep lines through his forehead and at the corners of his eyes.

"Was I that late?"

Andretti shook out his wrist, checked his watch, and hummed.

"It took me a while to find you," I said. "You didn't say where to come." It wasn't a total lie. I'd asked the man working the front desk, and he led me directly here. Dammit, I never asked his name. I should know all the staff.

A waiter, evidenced by blue slacks taking over the shorts in his uniform, pulled out a chair for me. He showed me a wine bottle's label, but I waved it off. "Old Fashioned, please."

"Excellent, sir."

I sat back in the chair, leaning into the soft support behind the cloth. "You seem very eager to get started, Mister Andretti."

He chuckled, exposing a perfect row of white teeth. "Please, my gastroenterologist calls me Mister Andretti."

"What shall it be, then? Marco?"

"My mother calls me Marco. Andretti will do. Yes, I am eager. Quite eager."

The waiter returned with my drink in a rocks glass that looked like a square twisted an eighth turn. A crystal clear ice cube of the same shape filled most of the glass, along with an orange peel.

"Thank you. What's your name?"

"Carmelo, sir."

"You don't have to call me sir, just Matteo."

He smiled and returned to his station by the kitchen door. Carmelo, I'd remember him by his longer, curly hair with an undercut, thin lips, and ears gauged a half inch.

Andretti leaned forward, lacing his fingers. "Mister Demetriou, I understand you are not accustomed to your position, but I urge you to maintain a level of professionalism with the staff. Getting too familiar with some may create an air of favoritism."

I already flushed any chance of professionalism down the bathtub drain. "Understood," I said. Letting the ice melt for a moment, I took the dark cherries skewered by a silver pin straddling the glass's top, and bit one off.

"Let's start, then," I said, finally wresting my gaze from Carmelo. "I still have some papers to sign, and then there's the opening. What is there to say with the investors? Do we need to talk about finances? How's the soft launch going?"

Andretti held out his empty glass, and Carmelo immediately refilled it. "Saying only *some* papers is a severe understatement. Most of that can wait until after dinner. Thank you, Carmelo."

The waiter put a hand on the kitchen door, but I caught his grin when I held up the cherry stem tied in a perfect knot before he exited. What was Andretti just saying about professionalism?

Andretti cleared his throat and continued, speaking quietly. "For now, I wish to discuss a security matter with you that was inappropriate to discuss over the phone."

I spat out the second stem before I choked on it. Could this be something with my father? What did he know about that ChatSphere message? Rather than give anything away, I took the first sip of my Old Fashioned, letting the bourbon's bite mask my expression. Except, there was no bite. The liquor slid down my throat as smoothly as anything, warming as it went despite the ice. The rich, oaky bourbon cascaded over my palate, its robust character mellowed by the gentle caress of simple syrup. I held the glass up, taking in the subtle aroma of aged whiskey mingled with the zesty whisper of orange peel.

"What I showed you earlier was an aliased client list," said Andretti. "Your father was ever vigilant that the list never be printed intact. Above all the amenities of La Luce, client discretion is our top priority. If word spread of a conservative United States Supreme Court justice taking a holiday here with a Saudi prince, purely hypothetically speaking, we would attract a sort of publicity that would end us. As well-funded as La Luce may be, our clients could lock us in lawsuits until the sun burns out."

I nodded, taking another slow sip. Goddamn. I'd become an alcoholic by the week's end here.

"When we arrived, the head of IT, Mister Manoli Petras, came to me immediately. The mainframe was breached last night, and a hard copy of the opening client list, which includes those present for the soft launch, was printed. All staff have been interviewed, and everyone with the proper access is accounted for with solid alibis confirmed with video surveillance, as much as there is."

I worked with spreadsheets for the last ten years but knew nothing about computer security. So, this wasn't about my physical well-being. A minor relief. "How do they know a printout was made? Are they watching the file?"

"IT has scheduled tasks to scan for suspicious activity. I admit I have some minor blame for this. I had them set up your account a week ago but have kept it inactive until today. Today, midnight, not when we arrived. Someone entered the system as you at 12:08 am, one minute after the last scheduled system scan. They had nineteen minutes to print the list and get away from the terminal before any alarms sounded."

I set down my glass, running a finger around the rim while I found my words. "This is an inside job. Someone knows the deepest workings of the system. Now that someone has a piece of paper worth a hundred million dollar resort." I ran a hand through my hair. "Do we know where it was printed? Where did they access the system?"

"Yes." Andretti set down his wine glass. "Suite 0-0-1. Your suite."

Four

Enzo

I STARED AT MY hands, watching how they shook. I'd lived in the same apartment in Bloomington, Minnesota, just a quick walk from the Taco Bell, for the last few years, most of that with a guy I'd love to forget. We moved to that shithole after an interrupted break-in at the last place. Waking up and stumbling to get a glass of water in the middle of the night, only to find two guys in the living room trying to steal my shitty TV left me scarred and feeling utterly unsafe in my home. I wanted to talk to someone, a professional, to help me deal with the fact that I couldn't be in the dark in my living room, but Pete told me to "Stop being a pussy." I ran, paid out the ass to break my lease, got a new job, and Pete somehow ended up with a key to the new place.

Those feelings trickled back to me now.

"Someone snuck into my suite this morning?" I watched the ice in my drink slip with a gentle clink as it melted.

"Try not to worry. The thief will not get away. I told you more as due process. They are still on the island," he told me, finishing his wine. "IT executed a full lockdown. No ships or planes have left the island, and all transmissions are being suppressed or fully monitored. I apologize for worrying you with this; I wanted it to come from me. This will be resolved."

All transmissions? Including cell traffic and chat apps? Would IT be able to trace the ChatSphere message? I forced another sip of my Old Fashioned. "What will happen when he's caught? Turn him over to the police?"

Andretti laughed and raised his empty glass to his lips, frowning when he saw me through the bottom. "Don't concern yourself with that."

I ran a finger around the lip of my glass again. Why was Andretti so insistent that I meet him, only to tell me things to worry me, then tell me not to worry? "No, I need more than that, Andretti. What's to stop someone else from getting into my suite?"

"The key I gave you is freshly reprogrammed. There are only two other copies. One on my ring," he patted his slacks pocket with a jingle. "The other is with maintenance."

That must have been how my luggage was delivered. "Until this is sorted out, I don't want maintenance to have a copy."

Andretti hummed, eyes running over me again. "If you insist. They will not be happy not to be allowed to do their jobs, but you're the boss."

"I'm fine with that. And do you need one?"

"I will if you share your father's forgetfulness for minor things." He drummed his fingers on the table once. "I will leave it in my office safe if it would make you feel better."

The lawyer knew the island's inner workings far better than I, obviously, but still, his flippant disregard for my safety grated on me. "Maybe I should stay in another room."

"No," he said immediately. "The owner must reside in the owner's suite. Doing otherwise would raise red flags that we do not need so close to the opening."

I shrugged. "Lie. If anyone asks, say I'm testing out other rooms for comfort."

"If you are concerned for your safety, your suite is the most secure."

"That can't be true. If La Luce is to host some of the biggest names in the world, there must—"

"There are secure villas on the south end of the resort, but moving you to one would be a vast overreaction."

This was my resort. I could stay where ever I damn well pleased. But, I could see only futility in continuing to fight him. "What about this list? How do we recover that?"

"We do nothing, Mister Demetriou. This is a matter for security. Unless you have some background with detective work or interrogation hidden in your lengthy CV, we will leave this to the..." He tipped his glass back, getting the last drop of wine collected there, and smacked his lips. "Professionals."

"There must be something I can do."

He shook his wrist, checking his watch. "It's just past four now. Dinner will be at 7:00 pm sharp. Herr Jensen, the tailor I mentioned earlier, was asking for you. He needs your measurements."

Great. I didn't want to return to my suite at that moment. "Where is the tailor?" I picked at my loose linen shirt, Lio's ankh catching the light as I did.

"Only a few minutes away. I'll call ahead so he knows to expect you." Andretti set down his glass to snap his fingers, a sharp, clear note. Carmelo immediately returned from the kitchen door. He was never far away, perhaps listening to everything. "Mister Demetriou needs a car." The waiter nodded and returned through the door.

"If it's so close, I can walk. I'll take care of that now."

Andretti called for Carmelo, who returned immediately. "Cancel the car and see Mister Demetriou to Herr Jensen's shop."

"Yes, sir. The one in Xemxmarina?"

"No, of course not," Andretti scoffed, then focused back on me. "I'll see you in a few hours. I've invited Signor Bianchi and Mister Romano to join us for dinner."

I mentally scanned through all the paperwork I'd seen over the last week, but my memory was far from perfect.

Andretti must have noticed my blank expression. "The general and service manager," he sighed. "I would invite Mister Petras, but I suspect he will still be... engaged with the security oversight."

Andretti provided dossiers about all the resort's important players, but being tossed in with them was far more overwhelming. Herrs, Signors, Misters, what else would there be?

I said my farewells, feeling like a child sent on a simple errand, but what more could I really do? I'd been on the island only a few hours and knew nothing about the operations.

Carmelo guided me back to the main lobby and offered to escort me to the tailor. "Herr Jensen is a genius," he said. "He makes all the uniforms. It feels like I'm wearing nothing."

I smirked, looking him over. "Is that so?"

He ran a hand across his narrow waist and over his ass. "How about that escort? To the shop?"

What was the hiring process like that the resort seemed solely populated by hot men eager to please? As much as I wanted to say yes, Andretti's words warning about professionalism rang through my brain. With difficulty, I declined Carmelo's offer while hoping I'd get another chance for him to "escort" me later.

Less than ten minutes of following discrete signs with the sun beating on my head, the boardwalk gave way to limestone pavers, and I looked up to a plaza of a half dozen shops. Each building stood apart, each painted and decorated with its individual themes, though the space still felt cohesive. Dolce Mare, the bakery with a half-empty window showcase of bread and fudge. A barber shop with no name, just a red and white pole beside the door. A pharmacy, by the alchemist's mortar and pestle sign, looked completely empty. La Luce was supposed to open in two weeks and didn't look ready from where I stood. The store with a placard reading "Jensen-Klassiker" in filigreed work like a thread's stitching looked plucked from Venice. I pushed in the heavy door with a single bell's jingle.

Inside, cool air greeted me, smelling of leather and shoe polish. Jackets and pants lined the walls, ranging from white to cream to blue and black, with a few splashes of colors and patterns. Racks of shirts and hats dotted the floor, creating a maze to a platform in the back surrounded by a ring of mirrors.

"Be right out!" Someone shouted from behind the heavy black curtains, followed by a crash. A man somewhere in his early thirties jumped through the curtain before I could call to offer help, snapping it closed behind him. He quickly combed his mop of hair with both hands, like someone caught doing something naughty, dark eyes wide with a toothy grin. He brushed off his long sleeves and straightened the fabric tape measure around his neck.

"How can I help?" he asked.

His frantic energy and mid-west accent threw me off, and I stumbled for the words. "Mister Andretti said you needed me."

His eyebrows raised half an inch.

"I'm Matteo. Er... Mister Demetriou, the new owner."

He gasped, stepping back with his hand raised almost defensively. "Yes, of course! You're here to see Herr Jensen." He shifted to the front counter to arrange the papers that already looked well-organized.

"I'm sorry, I assumed you were him."

He clapped once, and his smile returned. "I am, yes. Herr Enzo Jensen, at your service, Mister Demetriou." He bowed stiffly at the waist.

Not that I knew much about tailoring, but the fine stitching surrounding me seemed a stark juxtaposition to the wild young man in front of me. "Just Matteo is fine." Herr Jensen was a big name on the island, not staff, right?

"Well, Just Matteo, I'm Just Enzo." He stepped from behind the counter, eyes scanning over me as he circled, his fingers slipping over the tape measure around his neck, caressing it. His fingers brushed across my shoulders as he paced.

"Sorry, but why do you sound like you're from Chicago?" I asked.

"Because I am. Well, suburbs. And you sound like you're off the cast of Fargo. I'm sure you've had a standard fitting before?"

"I'm from New York." At least, I thought I still had most of my New York accent after thirty years in Minnesota. "And yes, I was fitted for a buddy's wedding about fifteen years ago but bought everything off the rack."

He tsked. "Mine are different. Anyone can craft clothes for a mannequin, a statue. My work is for a body in motion. I must explore how you move, not just run my tape up your inseam."

He stood before me, nearly my height, brown eyes flashing with a touch of gold, and ran a thumb down the chain around my neck, pulling Lio's ankh into the light. Enzo's expression soured as he whispered, "Interesting accessory."

I plucked it from his fingers, tucking the ankh under my low neckline. Clearing my throat, I spoke slower, now hyper-aware of my accent. "Can we get started?"

Enzo's smile returned in a flash. He hopped back, jerking his hips in what might be considered a dance. "I need to see how you move. How low can you squat? How high can you kick?" He lashed out a leg for emphasis. "Can you swim, or will your swimwear only be for show?"

His energy, which initially felt infectious and lively, was starting to grate on me. "I don't see how I'll have time for all that right now," I said.

"No, of course not." Enzo pulled the tape measure from around his neck like he was pulling off a tie after a long day at work. He tossed it around my waist, then up across my chest. "32 and a very solid 42, right where I knew you'd be. The actual measuring is just a formality after so long in the business." He stepped behind me to measure my arm's length.

"How long is that? I expected someone double your age."

In front of me again, he waggled his thick eyebrows. "Age doesn't always mean experience, Matteo." He dropped to a knee and measured my inseam. The tailor for Brett's wedding took that measurement without anything that might be considered indecent. Meanwhile, the back of Enzo's hand rubbed against my balls enough that I wasn't sure if he was doing it on purpose or if he was just uncareful. Either way, I didn't stop him.

He jumped up, only inches from my nose. "Right where I knew you'd be. I'll leave a little extra space in the thigh and groin. It feels like you need it."

The touch was on purpose, then.

Enzo tossed the tape measure around his neck like it was a scarf. "You're the same measurements as your father. I can see some of him in you. The same dark eyes, dimple in the right cheek."

Whatever oddness I felt toward Enzo faded with that statement. "You knew him?"

"Of course." The tailor nodded, returning to the counter to jot a note. "I did a fitting for him, but he didn't like much of what I made. He was so traditional."

I glanced around the shop of very traditional island creams and formal blacks.

"If you don't mind me saying," he continued. "Your eyes are much kinder than his."

"Meaning what?"

Enzo hummed and looked me over, toe to crown, ignoring my question. "I'm looking forward to getting to know your body. I hope you'll like what I want to put on it."

The heavy-handed innuendo tied my tongue for a breath. "Professionally speaking?"

Enzo laughed and blew out a raspberry. "I'm nothing if not professional, Matteo. I'll have my people call your people to set up a time to lock ourselves in your suite when I can learn everything I need to about you. Now, fuck off and let me get to work." He waved me toward the shop's entrance with another wry grin.

I had a hundred questions for him about the resort, about my father, but a few seconds later, I stood in the heat and sun of the empty street, still feeling the ghost of his hand against my balls. I took my phone from my pocket, seeing I had over ninety minutes before dinner. Plenty of time to stroll back for a quick shower. The elevator key dug into my thigh, and I pulled that out to hold in my other hand.

Right, all that. Murder, conspiracies, and thieves.

My phone chimed with a notification from Chat-Sphere. I swiped into the message in a new thread. Rather than a number, it showed the sender as an error.

Unknown: Follow me.

I glanced up. I was no longer alone on the street. A man in the pink and blue resort uniform, clean-shaven under his wide straw hat, stood three stores down. Though I hadn't gotten a good view of the gardener across the pool earlier, I knew this was him, who had watched me beat my stress against the balcony's glass. He disappeared down an alley as soon as our eyes met.

Pushing my cell and elevator key back into my pockets, I hesitated. Wasn't I worried for my safety scant moments ago? But... I needed, at least wanted, answers to what was going on here; answers that wouldn't come if I ran away from a stranger possibly willing to give them. Besides, it was the middle of a beautiful, sunny day, the opposite of prime time to lure someone into danger.

I ran after him.

Five

Alec

I CHASED MY MYSTERY voyeur from the street to the next. Every time I turned a corner, he was waiting to vanish as soon as I came into view. How could anyone move so quickly and calmly when I was sweating through my linen shirt? Only the white sand beach lay between us and the Mediterranean Sea, dotted with cabanas, their blue and white canvas flutteringly lazily in the breeze. I caught sight of his pink shirt disappearing into one. I was there a ragged breath later, running into a brick wall.

A brick wall that caught me at the shoulder and hip to keep me from toppling over.

Jumping back, I took in his details as quickly as possible. He was shorter than me by a few inches, putting him at maybe 5'10". Extremely well-built, but in the way of someone who works for a living, not just the glamor muscles from the gym. He removed his hat, revealing a scar beside his left eye that cut through his eyebrow. Hazel eyes under full lashes, wavy blond hair pulled into a top knot, silver stud in his right ear.

"Who are you?" I asked.

"Alec," he said without hesitation.

"Alec... Do you have a last name?"

"You don't need to know that." His voice twanged with a Boston accent.

Forced mystery was a definite turnoff, but I managed not to leave right away. "Did you send me this message?" I fumbled for my phone, which seemed to sense my anxiety, and refused to recognize my thumbprint.

"Yes. I have something for you." He pulled a folded sheet of paper from the front pocket of his shorts.

I accepted and unfolded the crumpled page. Sixty or so names were printed along with a mess of digital artifacts and illegible symbols, making them difficult to read. "Is this...?" I let the question hang. The answer was too obvious.

Alec nodded. "The client list."

I shied a step from him. "So you're the thief."

Alec shot out a hand, grabbing the front of my shirt and pulling me toward him before I stepped back into the sun outside the cabana. This close, he smelled like coconut sunscreen. He waved the other hand over his head, then pointed two fingers at his eyes. "It's not that simple, Matteo." He nodded his smooth chin at the sheet, and I noticed the dark splotches at the bottom.

"Is this blood?" I wanted to toss the paper away in disgust, but I knew its value.

"Ten hours ago, I took that off a person IT security shot."

"Ten hours? Andretti made it sound like IT was still searching for the thief, hacker, whatever."

"They are, but they won't find him in Xemxmarina."

"The village?" I tucked the client list away in the pocket with my elevator key and rubbed my face with both hands. "Wait, who was shot?"

"That's more information than you need to know." Alec took a leather wallet from his other front pocket. He snapped it open, flashing an ID card with "INTERPOL" across the top. It was gone just as quickly. "We were hoping for your cooperation."

"Of course, why not? I only just got here, don't know where the laundry is yet, and Interpol is asking for my help. Did you send me the other message, too? Before you watched me jerk off?" The heat rose in my neck and cheeks.

Alec's eyes narrowed. "I only sent you the message to follow me. What was the other?"

"Nothing." Great, I was getting messages from multiple strangers. "You don't deny watching me?"

His thin lip twitched upward. "I have been surveilling you, waiting for a chance that we may speak." He shook his head, dispelling the smirk. "La Luce is complex. A resort this size takes the entire island to operate. For every one employee you see in pink and blue, another ten are working quietly elsewhere. Matteo," he took my shoulders in powerful yet gentle grips. I knew he could hurt me if he wanted to. "Interpol knows you are unaligned in any of the criminal activity here. We aren't asking you to do anything to endanger yourself. Now that you have the client list, know it's recovered, you just need to listen for any news about it, take note of any inconsistencies. Can you do that?"

Could I? Sure. Did I want to? Fuck no. I'm not even here long enough to get hungry and Interpol hands me a bloody piece of paper and asks me to help take down some criminal something on my island? Did they even have jurisdiction here?

"Why are you telling me this? Why should I trust you?"

Alec shrugged. "Trust or not, just don't work against me. You have the list. Use it as you see fit."

I circled him, sitting on the white chaise, one of three in the cabana. "I need to know more. Who printed the list? Who was shot?"

Alec sighed and sat across from me, lacing his fingers together between his knees. His left palm was wrapped with a gauze bandage. "We don't have a name yet. My partner was watching him, followed him to the owner's suite this morning. He tried to flee along the north coast with the client list in hand, as if he had a contact up there, but no one was waiting for him."

"If you were watching this person, you must know something about him."

Alec pursed his lips. "That's more than you need to know right now. Anyway, he couldn't get off the island. We were about to step in, offer aid in exchange for information, but IT caught up, and there was a firefight. My partner got the thief away while I returned here."

"Why is IT going around shooting people? Shouldn't they be maintaining servers?"

Alec waggled his hand back and forth. "IT and security run a blurred line here."

I took a breath to process the story. "The list was printed at midnight, and you've had it since the thief was shot ten hours ago. That means he was free for eight hours. You didn't step in sooner? It took IT that long to find him?"

Alec chuckled. "You haven't been to the north end of the island. It's a miracle to find anyone up there, in those tunnels."

"And this is the only copy of the list?"

He nodded. "That is the original and no copies were made, to the best of my knowledge."

The first notes of a migraine pulsed at my left temple. "This is a lot to take in, Alec. You must understand it's hard to trust anyone who's telling me to trust no one else." Lio's stubbled cheek came to mind, but I shook the image away. "Especially someone who quietly watched me jerk off."

"It would have broken protocol to look away." His hazel eyes twinkled. "You'd be surprised how much crime gets done by invoking a sense of modesty. It happens more than you'd think that a criminal negotiation starts with fucking, just so the cameras get switched off."

"Sounds like you watch people fuck often. Do you enjoy that?"

"All part of the job." Alec adjusted his blue shorts, drawing my eye to his bulge. Agent Alec of Interpol by way of Boston, how I wanted to touch that swelling, squeeze the head, and stroke the shaft.

What the fuck was wrong with me to keep thinking about sex while surrounded by danger? It had to be the temperature.

"If I help you, if I cooperate with Interpol, what do I get out of it?"

"Not going to prison isn't incentive enough?" Alec smiled, but I didn't match him. He cleared his throat. "We have no interest in the operation of La Luce. If we can work precisely here, with you helping or at least not hindering, the impact on activities will be minimal. Your grand opening will go off without anyone suspecting a thing."

"Coming from the guy involved in a shoot out this morning." My gaze ran over the tight fit of his pink polo. He might have been poured into it for how it molded to his abs and biceps, how his nipples stood out as perfect peaks to the mountains that were his pecs. My dick twitched once, stiffening, as eager as my conscious mind in my desire to strip that shirt off Alec, lean him back in the chaise, and see if he had any tan lines.

I coughed, forcing myself to focus.

"I have a dinner to get ready for. I'll see what I can do, but I'm no detective." Standing, I looked down at him, my near-full erection pointed inches from his face.

"I wouldn't ask for more," he said, and I noticed his gaze flick to my groin. "Take extra note around

Giacomo Barbieri, whom I'm sure you'll meet soon. We have reason to believe he was deeply involved in the theft, despite being one of the investors."

"Barbieri?"

Alec nodded. "Yeah, watch out, he's a real cunt. I'll contact you within a few days, but I'll be watching. Give me some signal if you want to meet sooner."

I nodded. Saying thank you felt inappropriate at the moment.

Alec took my hand as I turned to leave the cabana, his calloused fingers wrapping mine, reminding me of his raw strength. "Be careful, Matteo."

"You too."

He squeezed once, then released.

I took a few steps into the sun and glanced back. Alec was gone. My phone told me I had an hour until dinner. La Luce's main building could be seen from anywhere in the resort, but I still followed the signs rather than get lost in some failed shortcut through the tight streets and paths.

Soon, I was back in the cool lobby. The only person in sight stood from the bench beside the elevators, grinning around that bit of stubble, and I felt a weight drop from my shoulders.

"We meet again, Mister Matteo." He pushed the elevator call button and picked up another garment bag from the bench, holding the hook over his shoulder.

"Not soon enough, Lio."

As I passed him, I ran my hand across his stomach, and we stepped into the elevator car.

Six

Quickie

"**I** BROUGHT YOU A change of clothes for dinner, Mister Matteo," Lio said. "I'm glad I did."

My linen shirt clung to me with sweat that had nothing to do with the climate, at least not completely. I took the elevator key from my pocket, careful not to draw attention to the client list folded around it as I did, and was satisfied with the soft click when I put it into the slot beside the penthouse button. As the doors closed, I breathed deeply, taking in Lio's woody, musky scent.

"You've had an interesting few hours," Lio said, tracing his free hand across my back, then rubbed his thumb against his fingers.

"You can say that." I thought to leave it there, but if I couldn't trust anyone on this island, I might as well sign La Luce over to Andretti and fly back to Minnesota. Maybe he was hoping I'd do exactly that. "I met Andretti for a drink, stopped in with Herr Jensen, and went out to see the beach."

The doors opened to my suite, the sun coming through the windows at a longer angle than when I'd left. I glanced back when I noticed Lio hadn't immediately followed me into the room. He stood in the elevator car with the garment bag in both hands, gray eyes wide. I might not have thought anything of it if it wasn't such a stark contrast to his confidence and eagerness a few hours ago. He looked smaller, deflated.

"Are you okay?" I asked.

Lio took a deep breath, his easy smile returning, and stepped forward. "What is your favorite drink, Mister Matteo?"

"Whiskey, bourbon. Specifically an Old Fashioned. Goddamn, that was the smoothest drink I've ever had." I stroked my throat, imagining the warmth as that first sip slid down.

"Sounds nice." He hung the garment bag on a hook beside the bed and unzipped it, fluffing the cotton and linen to let it breathe.

"What's yours? I bet you're a tequila shooter." I wandered close to the windows as I spoke, stepping out of my shoes as I did to feel the plush carpet between my toes. I scanned the balcony for my cum smear. I was pretty sure of where I'd been standing, from the viewing angle, to where Alec had been watching me, but the glass all looked clean. Either I was blind, or the sun had miraculously cleaned it. Or someone had been in before Andretti took the key back from maintenance. Was someone else watching to know it needed cleaning, or was it a regular visit?

"I don't drink," Lio said close to my ear. He laced his fingers through mine and pulled me toward the mirrored hallway leading to the bathroom. "Let me help you get cleaned up for dinner."

"Is there a computer station in here?" I asked halfway down the hall.

Lio stumbled at my sudden question, opened the closet door to his left, closed that, and tried two on the right. He stepped aside on the last one, revealing a dark monitor in a fold-out station. A yellow pull bar across the front would probably unfurl the whole thing with a keyboard, trackball, and stool. I noted the printer tucked on a high shelf.

"Thanks. I don't know why I suddenly thought about that." I grinned and closed the mirrored door, holding back a cringe at seeing our reflection. Next to Lio's perfectly tanned complexion and godly build, I looked in desperate need of Vitamin D injections with sweaty curls plastered to my forehead. My Greek blood barely showed through after so many long winters. What was the true story of my family that when I was ten, my mother moved us from New York state to Minnesota, while my father apparently moved to a Mediterranean paradise?

Lio nodded down the hall and tugged me toward the bathroom.

"I'm meeting with Signor Bianchi and Mister Romano over dinner. Can you tell me anything about them?" I started pulling off my shirt, and Lio was there immediately to help. So close, I just wanted to feel those lips on mine again. We could both climb into the tub and skip dinner.

With my sweaty shirt in hand, he stepped away to turn on the shower. "To be completely honest with you, Mister Matteo, Santiago Bianchi's a hard ass. I've never seen him smile, and he always has a clipboard in his hand, yelling about things not getting done. Elias Romano is just the opposite. He's so laid back but always gets everything done ahead of schedule." He spoke as he returned, his hands deftly working at my belt buckle. I'd never had a man do that when we weren't about to fuck, and my dick didn't know what to think about it.

"They sound like hard workers." I stepped out of my linen slacks, watching Lio fold them to sit on top of my shirt on the counter and thinking of anything to keep me from getting fully aroused.

The client list.

The wadded and bloodied bit of paper capable of taking down the resort was in those pants. My dick shriveled as I thought of how I might casually move the list elsewhere without drawing attention. Though, this was my moment to show absolute trust in Lio.

Not yet. He needed to earn just a bit more. I had to know what was between him and Enzo. Why did the tailor react as he did when he saw me wearing Lio's ankh? Why did Lio act as he did when I mentioned meeting Enzo?

I dropped my trunks as he returned for them, kicking them up with a foot and catching them with a grin to stand naked before Lio. Naked, save for his ankh necklace. His eyes washed over me, lust clear by how he bit his lower lip.

The shower was a work of beauty in itself. Large enough for four to comfortably go about their business, more if you weren't there for just business. Water and mist sprayed from six angles while also raining from the ceiling. I adjusted the temperature down two degrees with the touchpad on the wall and noticed the change immediately. The whole experience made me think of a car wash. A beautifully warm, perfectly balanced high and low-pressure car wash. Screw the tub, I could stay in here all day. Andretti had mentioned something about freshwater sources being a problem on the island, but he also said my father solved that.

"Have you been in here, Lio?"

"I have not," he said, watching me from the glass door. "It looks nice."

"It is. I'll get your back if you get mine." I poured a handful of shampoo into my hand from the rack on the back wall, lathering it through my curls, breathing in the richness of olive with a citrusy note of bergamot.

"I wouldn't want you to be late." Lio sounded farther away, but I couldn't open my eyes with suds in them.

"As you said, everyone on the island serves at my pleasure." I cringed at the wording. It sounded sexy coming from Lio. In my voice, I sounded like a Bond villain. "But you're right. I don't want to set a precedent like I think my time is worth more than theirs."

With the shampoo clear of my eyes, Lio was no longer watching me from the shower door. A surge of panic hit me, but I could see my undisturbed stack of clothes on the sink counter across the bathroom. Maybe he had to pee. I accelerated my shower, getting a few pumps of conditioner with a matching scent. Finishing that quickly, I reached for the body wash.

A solid arm slipped past mine, taking the bottle. Despite the water's heat, Lio's skin felt like fire against mine, his hairy, solid chest pressing against my back, his dick nuzzling the cleft of my ass.

"We have to be quick." His breath along my ear sent a shiver across the base of my skull.

I pressed back into him, one hand running along his hip to his thigh.

Arms wrapped around me, he pumped wash into his palm, thick and white, and lathered, filling the steamy air with the exotic depth of sandalwood and something sweeter, perhaps jasmine?

I shrank in his arms, molding into him. His hands worked over my chest and arms, touching every inch of my skin. His cock stiffened against my ass, pressing against me, and it took all my willpower not to reach back to guide it home. I wasn't much of a bottom, but I would be for Lio in that moment. He worked across my stomach, then paused for a fresh pump of soap before moving on.

Both hands slid along my hips, between my legs, and gently cupped my balls on the way back up. He repeated it twice more with growing aggression before wrapping his left arm across my chest, holding me tight as his right hand worked my shaft in an unfamiliar rhythm. Unfamiliar but effective.

My knees quaked once, and Lio shifted back, releasing my cock and his arm around me to work his hands across my back, down to my ass.

One more pump of wash.

He dropped to a squat behind me, working his hands down each leg and motioning for me to raise one foot at a time. He stood. I was almost clean.

One more pump.

Strong, calloused hands gripped my ass, slipping up my crack. He slid a hand around my stomach, locking us together as one finger found my hole, teasing it, swirling around it, pressuring it.

If not for his iron grip, I would have buckled with a gasp when he pushed a finger inside me.

I leaned forward, inviting him to do as he pleased.

Yeah, there was no way I could bring up Enzo now.

He dropped to a squat again, hands spreading my cheeks, and his tongue shot out, driving me forward half a step. I braced a hand on the granite wall, nearly blind from the cascade running across my head. Lio guided my hand that reached back for his shoulder to my dick, and I took the hint. The stimulation overwhelmed me from my prostrate up to the crown of my head, and I shot for the second time in a few hours.

He stood as I turned. Standing chest to chest, staring into those gorgeous gray eyes, I reached between us to take his cock in my hand. Of the dozens of men I'd been with, none drove me to the animal lust I felt at that moment. The resort could burn around me as long as I had this rock-hard cock in me. My other hand shot behind his head, pulling him forward to kiss, fast and passionate. His tongue brushed against mine, pushing into my mouth with the same energy as I gave him.

Lio pulled his head back and put a hand on his cock to stop my motion. He grinned with a tiny moan. "There will be time enough for that later, Mister Matteo."

I huffed, feeling like Veruca Salt exclaiming, "But I want a golden goose now!" Except the golden goose was Lio's uncut cock. Not just his dick. His hairy chest, strong arms, kissable lips, those eyes I'd like to lose myself in.

He turned off the water and promised to save himself for after dinner. This would be the longest meal in my life. Andretti told me to relax and enjoy my time with the amenities, but I don't think he meant this.

Stepping from the shower, I immediately noticed my clothes scattered on the floor beside the counter.

Seven

Dinner

RUSHING TO THE SCATTERED clothes, I tore through the right front pocket. Empty. Cold sweat trickled down my back as I shoved my hand in the other pocket, taking out my cell phone and a waded scrap of paper. I unfolded it enough to see a blood stain before shoving it away. I had a clear memory of putting the client list in the pocket with the elevator key. Except, where was the elevator key? Right, I set it on the table by the window. Maybe I took the list out of my pocket and put it back in the other while gazing out to the balcony.

"Something wrong, Mister Matteo?"

Lio held a fluffy towel in each hand, making no effort at modesty. I soaked up the sight of him, his hairy chest and stomach, his thick erection pointing at me from a nest of dark pubes, his thighs corded with muscle.

He looked the model of innocence, standing naked before me, eyes wide with worry. It made no sense. Why? Why was he so interested in me? Was it all to win the role as my valet?

I forced a grin and dropped my pants, but I left my phone in my hand. "It's nothing," I lied. "I thought I heard my phone ring."

Lio closed the space between us, flung one towel around his neck, and tossed the other around me to pull me to his chest. His shaft pressed against me. His eyes locked on mine as he worked the towel across my back.

I melted forward, wanting little more than to remain safe in his arms for the rest of the night or as long as needed. My hands moved on their own, slipping along his hips and across his lower back. My rational mind understood that I knew nothing more about Lio than I did Enzo or Alec; that I'd spent far more hours with Andretti. Yet here I was, naked in his embrace and not wanting to leave.

"You'll be late, Mister Matteo." His fingers massaged my scalp through the towel.

I looked at my phone again—twenty-one minutes to dinner. There was barely enough time to get to the restaurant, let alone dress and do something with my hair. I took the towel from him, and he went to work with the other on himself. "Could you get the set of clothes you just brought?" I asked.

Lio tied his towel low around his waist, stooped to gather up my things from the floor, took three steps toward the door, and turned with the client list between his index and middle fingers.

"Oh, thank you," I said, plucking the paper from his hand with a grin. "Don't want to wash that." I set the list on the counter and my phone on top of it with all the casualness I could muster. Combing my fingers through my curls, I got it to something presentable by the time Lio returned.

He said nothing about the list or the dinner to come, only helped me put on the clothes. The slacks were a stormy gray, and he left enough buttons undone on the navy blue shirt with tiny pink fish to show the ankh pendant hanging from its necklace. He slipped back into his uniform while I did a final hair check.

"Shall I call again after dinner, Mister Matteo?" he asked, handing me a new pair of designer leather deck shoes.

"Sure, yeah. Give me your number."

He gave a wry grin. "None of the employees carry a phone while working. I could try back in a few hours."

Right, Lio was on the clock. He was on the clock when he delivered my clothes earlier, and while I was in the bathtub... "Or..." A plan started to form. "Would you like to stay here? Watch TV or whatever you like."

His smile deepened, creasing around his eyes. "I will ready your suite for your first night in your new home; put away your luggage and straighten the sheets."

Though I wasn't sure what he was offering—sex, companionship, or professional gain—I wasn't ready to say no to him. "One more thing." I took the elevator key from where I'd left it by the window and took the scrap of paper from my pocket. I rubbed my thumb across it for a heartbeat and shoved it back away. "Never mind."

Tearing myself from his embrace was difficult, and I still felt Lio's lips against mine as I entered the restaurant a few minutes later. Wearing a tailored three-piece suit and a carmine scarf around his throat, Andretti sat with two other men. Carmelo hovered over him, pouring from a bottle of red. As I made for the remaining chair, one of the men stood, tossed back his wavy, shoulder-length hair from a wide smile, and raised a martini glass to me. His rustic white and gray shirt left most of the buttons undone, showing a chest shaved smooth draped with a handful of necklaces bearing tiny steel feathers, a stamped coin, and a twisted ring.

"Here he comes now," he said far louder than necessary in a thick Australian accent. He raised his glass a few inches higher, then downed the contents. "You must be Mister Demetriou." He blew out a long breath and hiccuped.

I returned the smile and took my seat. "Please, call me Matteo. You must be Elias Romano, service manager of this fine resort."

"Eli." He mumbled a thanks to Carmelo for refreshing his beverage from a shaker.

"Hello again, Andretti." I nodded to the lawyer and held back a gasp when I focused fully on the last man. His dark blue eyes, creased at the corners, bore into me. I put him in his early fifties by how his manicured beard and impeccably quaffed hair were tinged with salt at the temples and chin. He wore a dark green, single-breasted vest with brass buttons over a cream shirt, sleeves cuffed at the elbows, and he rolled a rocks glass between his thumb and middle finger. Everything about him spoke to a carefully curated appearance. The refined older gentleman. What the kids might call "daddy as fuck." Not me, surely, but I wouldn't deny how my eye lingered on him.

"I hope this tardiness won't be an ongoing trait." His words were crisp and perfectly articulated.

Heat flushed across my neck. "Not at all. I'm still getting my bearings. You must be my general manager, Signor Santiago Bianchi."

He raised his glass, pausing for the briefest salute, and sipped the amber drink. I shook from his penetrating stare when Carmelo placed a glass before me, another of the delectable Old Fashioneds. Santiago's left eyebrow raised an eighth of an inch.

"My father always said you could never trust a man who doesn't drink whiskey. He shot himself when he was forty-three. Cheers." Santiago raised his glass again.

I lifted mine but had no words to add to the awkward toast.

Andretti cleared his throat and pulled four packs of spiral-bound papers from his briefcase, putting one in front of each of us. "On that note, here are the latest operational updates compiled by Signor Bianchi. Let's get to business."

Eli pushed his packet away and raised his glass a little too quickly, sloshing drink over his hand. "There's no business without the opening. That's the only thing we should be blabbing about here." He noticed the spilled drink and fumbled with his cloth napkin.

Andretti snapped his fingers. "A tonic water for Mister Romano." He reached across the table and wrestled the glass from the service manager.

"Top of business for me," I said, "is an update about the earlier matter. Has IT made any headway?"

Andretti turned to me with a forced grin. "That is privileged information, Mister Demetriou." His gaze flicked to the drunkard batting his eyes at Carmelo, wishing for another drink.

"Should there be secrets amongst the core resort staff?" I asked.

"Very well." Andretti leaned back, tugging at the hem of his dark jacket. "Carmelo, check on the first course."

The waiter nodded and excused himself.

"I would thank you for greater discretion, Mister Demetriou," Andretti said through clenched teeth when the kitchen door closed. "The four of us may be core resort staff, but the waiters and gardeners are not." He leaned back, and his shoulders relaxed. "No. IT is no closer to recovering the list."

"I should have replaced Petras years ago," said Santiago, swirling his glass in front of his nose. "He says his team shot a man and still couldn't recover anything. Incompetence."

So Alec was telling the truth. "They shot someone? You left that out earlier, Andretti." I lifted my drink to my lips, breathing in that whisper of orange peel. I hoped the others viewed my casual acceptance of hearing about a gunfight as an air of nonchalance rather than trying to catch one in a lie.

Andretti waved his fingers, dismissing my comment. "It is unreasonable to anticipate that every detail, however minute, will be conveyed to you instantaneously."

"You think that's minutia? You told me about the theft as soon as you knew," I said. "I hardly think a shootout falls under minor delays to hear about days later. You should have told me."

Eli slapped the table. "Never you worry, Matteo. They won't get away in Xemxmarina. Hey, that almost rhymes. At least it almost did in my head." He chuckled to himself.

Andretti leaned forward, steepling his fingers. "On what basis do you surmise that the perpetrator sought refuge in the village?"

Eli flopped back in his chair and raised his hands over his head. "This is a resort focused on service, yes? And who's in charge of that?" He pointed down at himself. "You should know better, Andretti. Every boy in little blue shorts reports to me. Forget the state-of-the-art surveillance systems and kilometers of magnetic tape that never seem to work; I'm the eyes and ears around here." He ran both hands through his hair, shook it out, and crossed his arms with a gloating grin.

Andretti might have tried withholding information, but the other two were casual enough about the matter to cast any suspicions from them.

"Speaking of," Eli continued with a wink. "I've put together a little event in your honor tomorrow afternoon, Matteo. I hope you can make it since everyone has already said they'll be there to meet you."

Shit. Everyone wanting to meet me? That sounded miserable. "Very considerate of you, Eli. Thank you. That sounds lovely."

The kitchen door opened, and Carmelo entered with a tray of plated salads. For everything else about La Luce, I'd hoped for something grander as a first course than what they had at Texas Roadhouse.

"That reminds me," Eli said, leaning back for Carmelo to put a plate in front of him. "I had an appointment with Ricci last week, Doctor Ricci. You haven't met him yet, Matteo. He's the only doctor on the island. At least the only licensed one. He's very thorough." He mimed two fingers thrusting upward. "He told me, quite suddenly, that I have to stop masturbating. Could you believe the nerve? I called him a bleeding wowser and told him it was perfectly natural. Everyone does it, and everyone should do it." He paused to crunch a single crouton. "He told me to at least wait until after the examination."

I snorted into my drink, and Carmelo fled to the kitchen with a hand over his mouth.

"Did you come up with that yourself, Eli?" Santiago asked with a twinkle in his eye.

"You caught me. No, I saw a video of Sigourney Weaver telling it. I'm paraphrasing, of course."

"How did anything remind you of that, Mister Romano?" asked Andretti.

"No reason, just part of the joke." Eli winked at me.

Andretti sighed and shuffled the greenery around his plate for a few seconds before pushing it aside to take up the binder again. "Please direct your attention to page seven, where we shall examine the recent performance metrics of the desalination plant. While the figures have not reached a level of immediate concern, it is noteworthy that they are persistently underperforming relative to our projected outputs. Herr Albrecht will have more to say on the matter at the investor meeting, but I thought to give some advanced notice."

"Before that, I have a question." The others focused on me. Even Carmelo looked from the corner of his eye from where he refilled Andretti's red wine. Bleary-eyed Eli looked a little relieved for a reason not to look at the book of tight text and charts just yet. I set down my salad fork and took up my glass. "You all are well aware that I never knew my father. I had not heard from him in decades. To help me process events, for my closure, could you tell me how he passed?"

"Your father was diagnosed with ALS," said Andretti.

Eli rolled his eyes with a loud scoff, and the lawyer shot him a look that could have lit a candle.

"What's that about?" I asked.

"Rafael Demetriou," said Santiago, as even as ever, "jumped from the north lighthouse."

"Allegedly," Eli added.

Andretti tapped a finger on the table. "The last confirmed sighting of your father was as he entered the lighthouse. Tragically, no remains were recovered, which is not unexpected given the treacherous waters on the island's northern coastline."

The northern coastline, where the thief fled with the client list, hoping to meet up with a means of escaping the island. Where Alec intersected him. I'd have to see this part of the island soon.

"What does that have to do with ALS?" I asked.

"ALS did not kill him, but he would be alive if not for it," said Andretti. "Mister Demetriou left behind a written testament, elucidating the extreme suffering and inevitability of his illness and expressing his explicit desire to bequeath his estate to you."

"And here you are, Matteo!" Eli exclaimed.

"Here I am."

My father was in such pain that he dashed himself on the rocks to be carried off by sharks or squid. This was a private island that may or may not be associated with a sovereign nation. Did the last will and testament of a man who killed himself really matter here? Andretti, Santiago, Eli, Petras, and whoever else could have as easily swept that under the rug and taken control of La Luce without ever reaching out to me. So, why did they? Did they hold such great esteem for my old man's wishes? Were the legal documents ironclad?

The ChatSphere message came back to me. "Your father was murdered." Right, of course. Someone else was in that lighthouse, and the others sitting around the table, picking at their salads, were hoping that someone would target me next. No, that seemed far-fetched. It would be simpler to negotiate with the murderer than to bring me in. Unless the murderer was still at large and they set me up as bait. What did the life of a nothing man from Minnesota mean to a resort courting billionaires? Maybe the person who killed my father was sitting at this table?

Carmelo served a seared tuna and asparagus dinner but used at least fifty words to describe the seasonings and preparation process. By the time I was picking at a scoop of vanilla gelato, Santiago was sipping an espresso, and Eli had another martini in hand, the sun had set, and my brain was mush from Andretti's droning about the resort's maintenance reports, insurance, liability, and intellectual property concerns, and finished with succession planning. Exhausting.

"Your father bequeathed La Luce to you, Mister Demetriou," he said. "It is imperative for the investors to understand the succession plan in the unfortunate event of your passing. This is a standard procedural inquiry, purely a matter of business and not intended to be morbid, gruesome, or alarming."

He could say nothing was alarming about the discussion, but when your beneficiary asks you to get life insurance, it's not a bad idea to research the smells of common poisons.

"You know I don't have anyone," I said.

Andretti hummed. "At this moment, ownership would fall to me in the event of tragedy. Your father opposed the formation of a board of directors. It would be judicious to reconsider this structure in light of current circumstances and for the continued prosperity of the estate."

"Makes sense." I was just nodding along with the lawyer at this point.

"I suspect the investors will be keen to the idea of a board, as Herr Jensen is the only one with a named heir. Should anything happen to any of them, their returns are forfeit without owning shares in the resort."

Enzo had an heir? Interesting. "You must be some lawyer to talk them into giving you money with only a promise to give it back."

"Your father did all the negotiating."

"Huh, I'm sad I didn't know him." I pushed back my chair and stood. Eli followed my lead, keeping a hand on the table to steady himself. "The jet lag and warm air have done me in. I'm calling it an early night."

Andretti heaved a deep, slow breath, staring at me with exhausted eyes. "I told you to relax and enjoy La Luce, but we should spend the time preparing. Meet me here at two tomorrow afternoon." He tapped the table twice to punctuate his request.

"My party's at two," said Eli.

Andretti closed his eyes with a slow sigh. "Very well. Meet me at one, and I promise not to keep you."

"One o'clock, got it. Gentlemen, it was a pleasure to meet you both. I look forward to us working together to see La Luce's full potential."

Santiago rose to crush my hand in his. Eli looked ready to hug but settled for a handshake. Andretti only nodded. Taking my spiral-bound notes and reports, I flashed Carmelo a smile and turned from the table.

The warm night air buzzed with the murmuring drone of insects and the distant crash of the Mediterranean Sea. Gentle lights illuminated the path toward the resort's main structure, to my suite, to Lio. Though I tried to remain vigilant on the short walk, my mind wandered with what I'd learned at dinner. My father's alleged suicide, Eli's red-rimmed eyes everywhere, Andretti withholding information, and Santiago might actually be a cool guy to hang out with over drinks.

A dazzle against a waist-high boulder lining the path caught my attention, and I paused to examine it; looking like a smeared handprint. I touched it, pulling back to rub the still-wet... blood. Beyond the boulder, lit by the rising quarter moon, was a raked zen garden surrounded by a low wall of fragrant white jasmine. Lying face-down in the center of the zen garden, in a dark pool, was a well-dressed body.

Eight

Herr Jensen

SHOUTING FOR HELP, I clambered between the boulders lining the walkway, skidding to my knees in the tiny rocks beside the body. He faced away from me, so I put two fingers to his neck like they do on all the crime shows. The tremble in my arm, combined with the thundering of blood through my ears, made that pointless. I yelled again, thought I heard some reply, and carefully pulled him toward me, to his back. Though I didn't recognize him, there was something familiar about the older gentleman with white hair slicked back, matted with blood, and a thick, well-groomed beard to match. Blood soaked the left side of his face and down the sleeve of his cotton shirt.

Someone yelled in the distance, and I cried out, "Over here! Call an ambulance!" What emergency services were available within the resort? "Get the doctor!"

I tried again for a pulse, fumbling with hands coated in blood. With the amount of it draining into the stones, I held no hope of finding one but still tried.

His large leather wallet poked from an inside breast pocket, and I pulled it free, hoping for some identification to tell me who this man was. Something else fell out of it, moonlight catching on silver. I picked the delicate chain from the pool of blood.

The shouts were nearer.

The wallet and identification were dashed from my mind when I held the chain up to the meager light. A pendant hung near the end, snagged on the clasp—an ankh. Like a man possessed, I pocketed it and shoved the wallet back where I'd taken it.

Flashlights bobbed down the path. A moment later, Andretti gave me a handkerchief and offered to escort me back for coffee as Santiago examined the body. Chaos swirled in heavy sodium lights that flicked on from unseen sources disguised in the trees, bathing the world in harsh radiance.

"Return to the restaurant or your suite, Mister Demetriou," said Andretti, holding me by the elbows to keep me faced away from the gruesome scene.

"What the fuck, Andretti! A man is dead, murdered. I'm not going anywhere until we know what happened." I handed him back the handkerchief stained with blood, and he offered an individually wrapped wet wipe. As much as I scrubbed, I felt the man's blood cooling on my skin.

He gripped my elbows hard. "Do not use that word, Mister Demetriou. Herr Jensen was a master with the needle but unsteady on his feet. Unless we find otherwise, we assume he slipped on a rock."

"Herr Jensen? No, I met Enzo a few hours ago at his shop. He's a young guy." I glanced over my shoulder, seeing the scene now with more curiosity rather than horror.

Andretti's eyes narrowed, and he released me. "You met his son." He nodded his chin behind me, toward the body.

So this was the fabled tailor, the father of the lively young man I'd met a few hours ago.

A golf cart lurched to a stop, and a man hopped out carrying the black leather bag associated with doctors. He kneeled beside the body, checking the neck and wrist while Santiago spoke to him in a hushed tone. The doctor consulted his wristwatch, and the golf cart's driver pulled a sheet over the body.

The general manager approached us, wiping his hands on a blue cloth.

"This does not look good, Andretti. There are signs of a struggle," he said.

"Mister Demetriou was just telling me how he met with Mister Enzo Jensen this afternoon," said Andretti. "Within the resort." He barely moved his lips as he spoke the last words.

Santiago hummed. "Enzo would be the first for Petras to question, no matter where he was."

"I take it the two didn't get along?" I asked, dipping a hand into my pocket to touch the stolen silver necklace.

"That is putting it mildly," said Santiago. He turned to watch the doctor and assistant load the body into the golf cart.

"Shouldn't there be an investigation? Collect evidence before moving the body?" I asked.

"This is for the best. There are guests in the resort, and we cannot afford a crime scene. We will have enough questions to answer with the lights on. This isn't your American television," said Andretti. "Law and order look quite different on Isola di Luce."

"Meaning what? That there's none of either?"

Santiago folded his arms across his vest. "He has a point. Where is Petras? Security should be crawling over this place right now."

"Maybe they're all too busy shooting people on the beach," I murmured.

Andretti turned to me with a sigh. "Signor Bianchi and I will oversee matters here. I must insist you retire to your suite. Everything is only made more difficult by," he waved at the zen garden, "this."

"You are perfectly matched to your job, Andretti," said Santiago. "A man is dead, possibly murdered, and your focus never wavers."

The lawyer said nothing as he broke from us to approach the doctor sitting in his golf cart with a clipboard in his hand.

"May I escort you to your building?" Santiago asked. "Then I must find Petras. You may soon see a requisition request for a head of security in your weekly updates."

I nodded, giving the bloody patch in the zen garden a last look.

"What's the beef between Enzo and his father?" I asked, thinking of the tailor's reaction to seeing Lio's necklace on me. I'd have to pull the one I'd taken from his father out of my pocket to know if they were a match.

"Benedikt grew up in post-war Germany, his son in Chicago—literally two different worlds. The father worked only in conservative, classic fashion. The son wanted everything new and vibrant. The two were constantly butting heads, so I decided that only one at a time could be in the resort. It surprised me that you met with Enzo, as it is his father's shift."

"So it was just professional rivalry? Nothing else?"

Santiago looked at me and let his eyes drop to my chest, to Lio's ankh resting on its chain. "If you want to gossip, take a bottle of Popov to Eli's apartment, and you will know everyone's dirty secrets."

With the sodium lights behind us, the insects and distant waves returned. Stars swarmed the sky, with the Milky Way faintly visible as a band cutting across the heavens. Despite the storm I'd landed in, I could see the romantic appeal of this paradise island. It was almost enough to overlook that a man might have been murdered a hundred paces down the path.

"It'll be a long, dark night," Santiago whispered, barely audible. He paused walking, rubbing a hand across his face. "Benedikt was a staple here for decades. He..." Santiago wiped his palm across his eyes and down his mouth, then waved for us to keep moving. "Anyway, I don't deal in gossip and rumors."

"It's not idle gossip if something between them led to..." I pointed back down the path, glancing back to see the sodium lights visible through the gaps between trees and buildings. My hand trembled as the image came to me, of Benedikt's face soaked in his blood as I rolled him over. I shook my fingers into a fist to quiet them.

We stopped at the marble columns framing the front entrance to the main building with the fans blowing their pleasant mist. "That is my point, Matteo. Both Jensens worked at full productivity when one was in the resort and the other in their shop in Xemxmarina. Splitting them up worked, so the matter was resolved. They had their differences, but, well, you met him. Do you really think Enzo is capable of such a thing?"

Did I? I met Enzo for the quickest of periods. My brief vignette was nowhere near enough to form an actual opinion of the man, much less theorize what he was capable of. I wasn't the best judge of character on my best day, which was not today.

I wanted to ask more about my father or the resort's history, but I could barely keep my eyes open. "Well, thank you, Santiago."

He nodded. "I am off to find and throttle a security manager." He turned, then turned right back. "Metaphorically, that is not an admission of premeditation."

In the lobby, I grinned at the man behind the desk but couldn't bring myself to converse. I'd learned enough names for one day. With my back to him, I hit the elevator button and dug the deceased Herr

Jensen's necklace from my pocket. Holding it beside the one hanging against my chest, other than the blood, they were a perfect match. The chain styles were not identical, though. Lio's was slightly heavier weight.

The doors opened with a gentle chime. Lio grinned at me from the car, barefoot, wearing only his tight blue shorts and holding an empty ice bucket.

"You're early, Mister Matteo."

Nine

Ankh

WORDS WERE IMPOSSIBLE FOR the moment. I could only stare at Lio's perfection in the gentle light of the elevator car, his reflection multiplied in the mirrors. His gaze slid to Herr Jensen's necklace, and I tucked that away in a pocket.

My hand was shaking again, and I tightened it to a fist before stretching my fingers. I hoped this wasn't the start of a nervous tick.

"Lio, hi. Yes. Andretti's dinner became an overview of all island operations. I told him I need sleep. I..." What more should I tell him? Andretti chided me about controlling privileged information. Something this big, the death of a major player in the resort, would get out quickly, but Andretti and Santiago might want to control the narrative. What about the necklace, though?

"I took some liberties putting away your things. I hope you don't mind. You were out of ice." He raised the bucket in his grip.

"Do we need ice?"

"It's always nice to have on hand. The ice maker in your freezer was switched off."

Taking the elevator key from my pocket, I stepped in beside him. "You would have been stuck." I inserted the key and pressed the penthouse button.

He rubbed his temple. "I'd forgotten. Did something happen outside? I saw the heavy lights a little ways out."

He'd learn I was the one to find Herr Jensen. If I didn't tell him right now, I might as well write him off. If I didn't trust him with the knowledge, why should he trust me? But... Why? Why Lio? Anything I felt or wanted to feel towards Lio was nothing more than an ineffable vibe; something in the thin worry line creasing his forehead making me want to draw him into my world.

"Someone died. Santiago suspects foul play."

The doors opened to my suite. Lit by softer illumination and dotted with scented candles, it felt cozier than it had in the day's full sun. I tried to ignore it, refocusing on the grim conversation.

Lio stepped into the room, setting the empty ice bucket on the nearest horizontal surface. "Who?"

"Benedikt Jensen."

Lio clutched a hand to his bare chest, staggering a step to the side.

"You knew him?"

"Everyone did. Who would want to harm him?"

"Santiago is hoping Petras will be able to answer that. Meanwhile..." I couldn't take not knowing, so I dug the necklace from my pocket, dangling the ankh between us. I held up the one against my chest, making it clear that I'd noticed the coincidence. "Could you explain this?"

Emotion danced across his eyes, but I couldn't tell if it was shock, sadness, or fear. Lio lurched forward, snagging the necklace from me, holding it close to his nose with a thumb rubbing along the ankh's curves. "Where did you get this?"

"I found Herr Jensen. I... I don't know why, but I took this from him before anyone else arrived."

Lio closed the necklace in a tight fist. "You should not have done that, Mister Matteo." He turned away before I could read his expression.

"I need to know right now, Lio. Why did you give me a necklace identical to what I found on a dead man?"

"He told me he destroyed it," Lio whispered. He faced away from me, but I could tell he was staring down at the necklace in his palm.

"What's going on, Lio?"

He straightened, rubbed a palm across his face, and stepped to the couch, turning and leaning against its back. He looked smaller, diminished, like he had when I mentioned Enzo to him earlier as he stood in the elevator. "I'm sure you can assume."

"I'd rather not." Stepping out of my deck shoes, I moved in front of him and unclasped the chain from my neck. "What was there between you and Benedikt?"

Lio looked up, his gray eyes glistening. "He was my patron. I had nothing when I came to Isola di Luce two years ago, and Benedikt took me in. He was so kind. At least, at first. His son, Enzo, as you can imagine, hates me. He always had a strained relationship with his father. Then, I entered their world. I ended my arrangement with Benedikt almost a year ago, but it's... lingered."

I thought it odd that Lio would find me attractive, being almost twice his age, but Benedikt Jensen had to have at least another twenty years on me. "You two were intimate?"

Lio shook his head, then shrugged. "Do you want to know the details?"

"Yes and no? Your sexual history is yours to share or keep."

"Benedikt liked to watch. I would do chores around his villa, or he would invite someone for me to sleep with. It was the perfect arrangement for months. What young man could be unhappy in a life filled with luxury and sex?"

I nodded, agreeing.

Lio continued. "Eventually, I wanted more. I gave him the necklace as a token of that, and he rejected me, saying he wanted to keep things as they were. I asked for the necklace back, but he refused, said he'd destroy it, and I left. But we live and work on this small island and cannot avoid each other. After a few months, he wanted me back. I tried to remain steadfast, but I had moments of weakness."

Who hadn't been there, falling back into the comfortable, if toxic, arms of an ex? "I'd think the necklace would be a painful memory. Why were you wearing yours when I arrived?"

Lio tossed Benedikt's pendant on the end table beside the couch, but his eye lingered on it. "I've worn it since, changing what it means to me. It's a symbol of my rebirth on the island, of coming into my own."

That, I could understand. Take something hurtful and use it to strengthen yourself. "Why did you give it to me?"

He padded forward, slipping his fingers into my pant's waistline to tug me nearer. "To pass that flame of rebirth on to you, Mister Matteo. I saw the passion within you, even if you may not see it yourself. You hold a profound sadness and a soul capable of greatness." His hands moved around my hips, pressing me against him. I felt his erection straining at his blue shorts.

No. What the fuck was in the air on this island? Someone murdered a man less than an hour ago, less than a half mile from here.

"You knew him better than most, so who do you think meant Benedikt harm?" I asked, repeating Lio's question back at him.

He loosened his hold on me. "Enzo. He would gain all the rights to clothe the elite that La Luce will attract, take full ownership of the villa south of Xemxmarina, and his father's share of the resort's profit."

"Solid motives." I placed my palms flat on Lio's chest, feeling his steady heartbeat. I still had lingering questions, but enough answered to make it through the first night. The connection with Enzo, Benedikt, and the necklace made sense. Petras would investigate and bring someone to justice, and the investors would be pleased. I only saw sleep in my future, lacking any energy to repay the kindness Lio showed me earlier. "There are supposed to be cameras all over this place. This'll be over within a few hours."

Lio snorted. "I wouldn't count on it."

I pushed back from him. "Why do you say that?"

"Only that I hear from the other staff that coverage is spotty. There was nothing pointed at the zen garden."

"Did I mention the zen garden?"

Lio's face scrunched to mirror my confusion. "Maybe you didn't, but I assumed by the lights."

I stared at him for a long beat, trying to recall my words but coming up with only a hazy blank. I shook it off. "Right, sorry, I need to sleep, Lio."

His lips parted with a smile as he brushed a palm against my cheek and through my hair. "There is nothing to be sorry for, Mister Matteo. I can hardly imagine the stress you are under."

He seemed to grin a little too easily for a man who had just learned his ex-lover or patron or whatever just died, maybe murdered, but I hardly felt capable of analyzing someone else's emotions. My eyes burned, just trying to keep them open.

"May I stay?" He took one of my hands in both of his, taking the ankh necklace from me and holding the chain taut by the clasps.

I bowed my head for him to replace the necklace. "Fair warning, I snore."

"You won't after how relaxed I'll make you." His hands found my belt, tugging it loose without taking his eyes from mine. He moved up my shirt next, popping the buttons and pushing it over my shoulders. Close enough for his chest hair to mingle with mine, Lio's lips found my collarbone, sending shivers down my arms when they brushed my neck. His breath tickled my ear. "I told you I would save myself for after dinner."

Oh, I hadn't forgotten.

His hand shot down my front, yanking me toward the bed. With my knees pressed against the sheets, he gently urged me back with his palms flat on my chest. Never breaking contact with my skin, he slid to tug at my waistband, sliding my pants to my knees before my hips touched the thread count. Everything came off with a smooth motion down my legs, hooking my ankles and pulling them up onto the bed. I lie sprawled naked before him, again.

Lio popped the button of his fly and dug a thumb in his waist deep enough to show he wasn't wearing anything under those little blue shorts. "Are you sure you're so tired, Mister Matteo?"

I couldn't trust my words. I could only push backward toward the pillows and beckon him to join me.

Like a panther on the prowl... a lion... he crawled forward, pushing his knees between mine, moving up my body until his wrists were against my shoulders and thighs pressing my legs wide. His woody cologne overlapped with the jasmine bodywash from our earlier shower. His fingers glided across my stomach, down my arms, and I couldn't keep my hands off him, tracing the shadows cast by his muscle, over his tattoos.

He took my shaft in a hard grip, working it in a slow rhythm against his shorts. "I know what will help you relax." He shifted back, moving his hand across and under my balls. Standing on his knees, he worked his shorts down over wide thighs with no tan lines.

A minor horror struck me, fearing he expected me to bottom. Watching that god-sent erection bob at me while he wiggled his shorts around his ankles, I longed to feel him deep inside me, pressuring my prostate with a care and attention I'd never felt before, but he seemed eager to supply.

Just not right now.

Not after my travel and, Christ, the stress of this place! Andretti was upset with me, Enzo was just bizarre... fucking Interpol. A man was murdered a five-minute walk—

Lio pulled a thin bottle from the nightstand, snapping me back. He squeezed out a few drops, worked it between his hands, then spread his palms flat on my chest. The oil left a trail of warmth across my ribs to my hips. He ran once up my cock, rubbing the tip, and came again from the base.

"Lio, we shouldn't... after what..." My words were lost to the waves of pleasure making my legs twitch.

"That's why we should. We'll fall asleep thinking of this."

That didn't sound like proper psychological advice, but that little nagging voice was nothing compared to Lio sliding his thumb and middle finger up my length.

"I hope I can do this for you," he breathed. Before I could ask, he shifted his knees over my thighs. With a few more drops of warming lube in his palm, he sidled up to straddle my cock. "Don't hold back when you're ready."

He reached back to guide me and exhaled slowly as he eased downward.

"Take your time," I whispered, my hands on his hips.

He closed his eyes, focusing on his breathing. The pressure built... then I was in. Only an inch, but enough to pull a gasp from us both. He froze, hand slapping on my chest, eyes tight.

"You don't have to do this," I said, running my hand up his arm to cup his cheek.

"I want to. Just give me a moment."

Breathing in his nose and out his mouth, his shoulders relaxed over a ten count.

He nodded, as much to himself as to me, and eased down, not stopping until I had nothing left to give him. Even before he moved again, I was grateful he said it was okay if I didn't last long. The pressure of him surrounding me, the solidity of his pecs beneath the chest hair... the vulnerability in his eyes.

He rocked once, twice, shifting his hips to find the best angle. I worked his cock in time, knowing that would ease his pain. He leaned back, suddenly freezing with his eyes shot wide, mouth agape. "Fuck!"

"You don't—"

He rocked harder, faster, a wide grin spreading across his lips. "Do it, Mister Matteo. I want to feel you pump inside me."

Gun to my head, I couldn't stop if I wanted to. Any internal nagging about how I wouldn't have allowed things to get this far a week ago was gone with my first pulse. Lio pressed to my hips, his breath catching in his throat, and released it with his first spasm that I felt grip around my cock. He caught his load in a palm, redirecting it to pool on my belly, rather than blast across the sheets.

He rocked twice more before smoothly dismounting, tossing a leg off the bed, and leaning to press his lips to mine. "I'll get a towel."

Breathless, I could only reach for his arm as he slipped away, leaving me to stare blankly at the skylight over the bed.

Ten

Sign

DESPITE THE PAIN OF forcing my eyes open, closing them was worse. My mind filled the darkness with images of Herr Jensen staring up at me.

Lio lay sprawled beside me on his stomach, but the bed was so massive that only a hand touched my side. Taking my phone, I wiggled from under the sheets and closed the bathroom door behind me before turning on the light. I turned the water to just shy of scalding and scrubbed my hands in the sink with soap bursting with lemongrass. They were clean, but I still felt the ghost of Benedikt's blood on my fingers. I'd done the same last night while cleaning myself up after we'd fucked. Lio turned on the shower so we could take a quick rinse and made an awkward Lady Macbeth reference about me scrubbing in the sink. I'd chuckled, but that only served to highlight the inappropriateness of what we'd just done.

I'd never been so close to death. Attending a funeral was one thing, but to hold a body still warm and to find my hands coated in his blood? I could never prepare myself for that. No amount of jasmine-scented hand wash in the world could make me feel clean.

My brain was too active to sleep but too burnt out to do anything useful. Eventually, I dried my hands and sat on the toilet's cold lid. I noted the time, 3:12am, and brought up my last sudoku. I'd been working on it during the short flight onto the island this morning. Goddamn, that felt like another lifetime. Pinching and panning through the puzzle, tracing my notes of possibilities, I tried to find where I'd left off, but the numbers meant nothing to me.

Working on its own, my thumb swiped away sudoku, pulled up the recent app tray, and tapped the blue globe icon. The ChatSphere logo filled the screen and dissolved into my last message, the "Follow me." from Alec. I swiped back to go into the other recent chat.

+34 58 4115 7011: Your father was murdered. Trust no one.

I did a quick browser search and found that +34 was Spain's country code, but too many digits followed. Not that it meant anything. ChatSphere let you set your number with a username with no verification. The whole purpose of the app was anonymity.

Fuck it.

MinnGreekMatty: Who are you?

I snorted when I hit send. Having not used the app in so long, I'd forgotten my ridiculous username. No one called me Matty since Ma died.

I jerked with the buzzing response, almost dropping my phone. I must have fallen asleep on the toilet, it was 3:37.

+34 58 4115 7011: A friend

Some friend, not identifying himself, telling me wild accusations and leaving it at that.

MinnGreekMatty: What do you know about my father?

+34 58 4115 7011: Enough to know Andretti was lying.

Andretti? Fuck, this was someone from dinner! That was the only time the lawyer had mentioned my father, at least to me. It had only been the four of us.

MinnGreekMatty: Can we talk in person?

+34 58 4115 7011: Not about this.

MinnGreekMatty: I have to know about my father.

+34 58 4115 7011: Follow the investors and ask Andretti the right question.

Fucking cryptic bullshit.

MinnGreekMatty: What's the question?

+34 58 4115 7011: I can't say more.

Why was I sitting on the toilet talking circles with a faceless stranger when the hottest man I ever laid eyes upon was naked in my bed a few dozen paces away? I closed the app, put my phone into do not disturb, forced myself to pee, and rewashed my hands under scalding water.

Lio had rolled to his side. He didn't stir as I slid up against him, draping a hand against his stomach and burying my nose against his neck.

With the sun peeking over the distant horizon, I woke alone in an unfamiliar bed, tangled in sweaty sheets, momentarily frozen as I tried to remember where I was.

Yesterday filtered back to me like a movie played at high speed. All the faces and personalities I'd met. Everyone with their own past and agendas. Lio in the bath. Lio in the shower. Lio in bed. Herr Jensen's face, covered in blood, staring up at me, lifeless.

Silverware tinkled on dishes beyond the screen dividing the bedroom from the rest of the suite.

"Lio?"

Gathering the sheets around my waist, I peeked around the floral screen. Lio hovered over the dining table, wearing a fluffy blue robe, only coming to mid-thigh.

He stopped what he was doing and grinned at me. "I didn't mean to wake you, Mister Matteo."

Stepping out from the bed area, trailing the sheets behind me like a wedding train, I breathed deeply of the rich espresso, bacon, toast, and lemony hollandaise sauce. Lio was putting the final touches on arranging it all in a single setting to face out the window to the sea. "Did you make all this?" I asked, then noticed the wheeled cart.

His grin widened with a chuckle. "Oh no. I'm not much of a cook. I had the kitchen send something up." Lio offered me the seat and poured espresso into a tiny cup.

"Well, that's nice." A folded omelet drizzled with hollandaise and perfectly seared home fries filled my plate. Thick bacon and sliced toast took up another two smaller ones. Lio had arranged tiny jars of jams and spreads beside that. It all looked impeccably prepared and executed. "You're not joining me?"

"No. Mister Romano called an emergency meeting with all staff." He set my phone beside my fork. "I put this on the charger when I woke up."

"How did you know about the meeting without a phone of your own?"

"They told me when I called down for breakfast." Duh.

"I'm sure we know what that'll be about." I tapped my phone to see the time, 7:12 am, and noted it was at 88%. I trusted Lio, at least I wanted to. I'd better, after what we did last night. His hands running down my sides, that pain squeezing his face as he eased me into him... He wanted to please, at any cost. Something about that nagged at me. He wanted to perform a service, and while I was certainly not complaining, it lacked the passion and intimacy I'd normally thrive on. Maybe it was just that Lio was so different than any other man I'd met before.

"I'll see you before your meeting this afternoon, Mister Matteo. I recommend you stay in today. Rest. Recover from your jet lag." From behind, Lio placed one hand on my shoulder and kissed the top of my head. He slipped away before I could reach up to touch his fingers.

The elevator dinged, and I turned to catch him stepping in, still wearing the robe, but now I noticed his blue shorts under it. Where was the rest of his uniform? Not that he would turn an eye wearing that around La Luce, but where were the clothes he'd been wearing when I left for dinner?

He waved, and I raised my espresso cup in salute.

The doors closed, and he was gone.

"Fuck."

The fog shrouding last night was lifting, and I touched the ankh resting like an anchor on my chest. Lio had a motive to harm Herr Jensen, a shaky alibi, and was missing half his clothes. Were they covered in blood, wrapped around a murder weapon, buried somewhere close by?

But also, as short as it had lasted, that was one of the best lays I'd ever had.

I shot the espresso and poured another cup. Jet lag be damned.

Taking up my phone as I dug into the eggs, I thought to do some deeper research into the island's history, something I should have done a week ago, but a blue globe icon in my notification bar caught my attention—a message sent twenty minutes after the last.

> +34 58 4115 7011: You should try the private steam room. #4 is the best. Get settled before ten.

"Goddammit," I groaned and tossed my phone on the table. I needed help, someone who doesn't claim to have a part to play in the resort. One person came to mind, but he'd been exceedingly cryptic about how to reach him. "Give me some signal," he'd said. Swiping back to the other recent ChatSphere thread, I replied to "Follow me" with "u up?". A system message popped up the instant I hit send, telling me the recipient wasn't found.

Fine. Time for a more analog signal.

Tossing the sheets aside, I found Andretti's bound reports were where I'd left them last night beside the elevator, and ripped off the back page. I found a marker and tape in the kitchen, and a minute later, had an "X" taped on my window. If it worked for Fox Mulder, surely an Interpol agent from Boston would get my X-Files reference.

Now naked, I sat down to finish what I could manage of breakfast, barely tasting as I ate. My phone buzzed, interrupting my second forkful of home fries halfway to my mouth.

Andretti.

I stabbed the screen, answering on speaker. "Yeah?"

"Good, you're up. I waited as long as I could to call." He sounded out of breath, speaking quickly. "Petras fucked up."

I snatched the phone nearer. "What happened?"

"I'd kill him if I thought he was worth the paperwork."

"Andretti, what happened?"

"There are a half dozen cameras with useful angles to view last night's events."

"So you saw what happened with Herr Jensen?"

Andretti chuffed. "We certainly would. The matter would be done and settled by now. If any of the cameras were turned on."

Eleven

Vapore

"**T**HERE'S NOTHING, THEN?" I asked, standing and taking the phone off speaker.

"Nothing. Petras talked circles about rolling server restarts and applying security patches. He didn't seem the least bit phased or remorseful to be so negligent."

"What about Eli? What about his eyes and ears everywhere?"

"Mister Romano talks a lot. Try not to take too much stake in his words."

"What happens next?"

Andretti sighed loudly into his phone. "Stay put and await further word from me. Go through the reports again from last night. I will send a packet to prepare for the investor meeting tomorrow."

He hung up without a farewell.

I could shower, shave, and get ready for the day, but instead, I poured another cup of espresso and fell back into my chair.

With my brain buzzing from caffeine, I lost almost an hour avoiding thinking too hard about Andretti's phone call. With my feet propped up on the dining table, I downloaded all the addons for my language training app. Everyone so far had spoken English, but I'd have to learn something eventually. Rather than starting a lesson, I drifted back to my sudoku, keeping an eye on the notification bar for that damned blue globe. Even that didn't hold me for long, and I ended up staring out the window, letting my mind drift, hoping for some idea of what to do next.

I shook out of it, resigned that an idea of what I could do next wouldn't come to me on its own. La Luce was bedlam. No security, people sneaking around at all hours, murders, and everyone with their secret agendas. What tied me to it beyond my last name?

Lio had done as he said he would, putting away the contents of my luggage. My heart shot to my throat when I saw my pants from last night weren't wadded on the floor, but found them just as quickly in the hamper, the client list set on the table beside it, still folded.

Tugging on a loose pair of shorts, I stepped into the sun on the balcony, raising my face to its warmth. The very concept of La Luce twisted my gut—a resort for the ultra-rich and powerful to play out their fantasies before returning to their places as prime ministers, senators, and judges where they could pass laws to make my people's lives a living hell. Religious leaders and sports stars who vilified others for doing what they did in private. Where was the goodness in this place?

Maybe I could do something. Maybe I could compile enough blackmail to help nudge the world towards acceptance.

I snorted just thinking about it. I couldn't honestly think I'd have the resources to pull something like that off; the fantasy that fueled my imagination. Once La Luce was in full operation, the client lists would be worth a fortune, but this wasn't about money. This was so much more. This was power. Could I pull it off? No, it was only fantasy.

I shook my head and tugged my X from the window as I passed it. It was all pointless dreaming. I'd been on the island less than a day. I was in no position to guide the course of history from the shadows. Besides, it would only work once. As soon as one man's visit to La Luce was used for political persuasion, no one would ever come again. That one sell-out would have to be the absolute best to throw away this resort for it. Of course, La Luce could be just any other private island paradise after that, rebranded without the exclusivity.

I had time before the mystery number suggested I be in the steam room, so I tossed the shorts on my bed on the way to the shower. Bowing my head to the water just shy of scalding, it ran over my shoulders and down my back in rivers. Lathering a pump of lavender body wash, I began my mechanical bathing ritual, starting with my arms. My eyes were closed from the gentle spray but shot up when my hands reached my groin.

Why am I hard?

Sure, some memory of Lio lingered in the shower from yesterday, but...

I wrapped my hand around my cock, squeezing and bending it downward. Fuck, that felt good. I had the time, and starting the day with empty balls was never a bad idea. How many times had I cum since Lio walked into my suite yesterday? I was never like this in Minnesota. Though, to be fair, Minnesota didn't have Lios. It had Jims and Dougs. I started my rhythm and surprised myself when a finger slipped between my legs to push into myself to the first knuckle, then the second. Leaning my head against the stone wall, I imagined it was Lio behind me, and another finger pushed in. Not Lio; I felt weird about him right now. He hadn't run off with the client list and had eagerly mounted me a few hours ago before getting me breakfast, but that desire to serve felt... weird... Eli... Yeah... Nuzzling my ear, whispering nothings in that heavy Aussie accent, holding a martini in one hand and the other on my hip, smirking and making some inappropriate joke. The fantasy didn't last long before I shot onto the wall. I scooped it into my palm and wiped it off over the drain. I'd take up Santiago's suggestion and get a bottle of Popov for Eli Romano. How much of my fantasy could I make real?

Should I?

Twenty minutes later, after hiding the client list in the coin pocket of a pair of jeans in my dresser, I was studying a map in the lobby. La Luce had three locations marked with an icon like a steaming barrel, but all the names were in Italian. I knew a few phrases from when my mother would have her aunties over in New York, but that was thirty years ago. I compared the names for an embarrassingly long period before pulling out my phone to translate. Ice Bath, Turkish Bath, Stone Spa. *Il Bagno Turco*, here I come.

Heading in the same general direction as Enzo's shop, it was hard to miss the bathhouse with its blue-tiled dome roof and arches constructed from stacked sandstone. An arched entrance fifteen feet high led into the darkness beyond. My eyes adjusted quickly, passing through a thick curtain and around a corner to a dim changing room. A dozen lockers lined the far wall behind a bench, and another corner hid the toilets, urinals, and shower stalls.

If this mystery messenger wanted to meet me here, I may as well get into it. Opening the farthest locker, I found it was already stocked with two towels and a tray of soaps and lotions. I stripped, wrapped a towel around my waist, and put my phone on silent before going around the corner and through the other curtain leading deeper into the baths.

A steaming pool lined with blue marble dominated the room, lit by a shaft of light from the ceiling twenty-five feet overhead. Columns and supports created dark corners, nooks for consensual sin. I imagined the place in operation with sweaty men leaning back against the wall or lying on the cool stone, legs dangling in the warm water. Two men waded toward each other, slipping hands around the other's waist and pulling close for an aggressive kiss. Hands grip and fingers explore. A third man joins them.

I shook out of it, realizing my palm caressed my cock through the towel. Seriously, what was in the water here? I inhaled the rosewater and eucalyptus, hoping it might calm me.

I explored the outer edge of the baths, finding small alcoves that might fit two people. Three if you were close, which I'd bet was the intention. When I noticed the small Roman numerals just inside each, I found the one with "IV" in the darkest recess and settled on the cedar bench across from its entrance. I tried to look intimidating for the mystery man when he arrived, but I found that difficult when only wearing a towel around my waist that didn't reach my knees. Would he come? Why here? There had to be another place in the resort where we could meet.

My phone said it was just after ten when I heard a voice rising in the main chamber. Booming and deep, he spoke heavily accented Italian, overstressing the vowels, as he came nearer. When a second man spoke, softer and faster, it sounded like they were just outside the alcove. I caught a few words as the first man spoke again, though not enough to understand what they were discussing. Something about the softer man's voice was familiar. The first man moaned with his next reply.

Dropping to my hands and knees, I crawled across the dark alcove and peeked around the corner.

The man lying facedown on the marble beside the pool would be better called a bear. Not just in the sense of a large, hairy gay man, but the size and build of a grizzly. His arms, which might have been bigger than both my thighs, were crossed above his head, and I doubted two of me could touch hands around his chest. I would have remembered seeing him before wandering the resort as one of the guests. Maybe he was one of the investors. A smaller man kneeled between his legs, pumping lotion into his hands. He turned toward the grizzly, and I recognized those gauged ears and undercut.

The waiter.

Only wearing a towel, Carmelo gripped the bear's bare ass and worked upward with the experienced hands of a masseuse. In his uniform's long sleeves and pants, I hadn't seen the sleeve of tattoos down his left arm and across his chest. What looked like twisting vines traveled down his ribs, under the towel, and around his thigh. The huge man moaned and rumbled something in Italian that I was pretty sure translated to, "Fuck, that feels great." They spoke back and forth as I watched, unsure which of the two I'd rather be in that moment. The bear looked relaxed, and I wouldn't mind Carmelo between my thighs, but at the same time, I wondered what it would feel like to touch a man that massive.

My ears perked up when the bear said "La Luce," and Carmelo's response included my name. I strained to remember more phrases from the aunties, but it was impossible.

Wait, my phone! I literally just downloaded all my language education app extra content. I turned my phone's brightness down and opened the app.

Within a few clicks, the Italian conversation ten feet away was zipping across my screen in English.

"He seems like a nice enough guy, but it's too early to tell where he stands," said Carmelo.

"What's his type? Andretti or Romano?" said the bear. My app even color-coded the speakers. Well worth $14.99.

"Lio is said to have slept in his suite last night."

"Who?"

"Lio Carbone, one of the porters."

"Young?"

"And attractive."

The bear sighed. "So he likes them young and attractive. You are young and attractive, Carmelo. Why are you still wearing that towel?"

Carmelo untucked and tossed it away. His thin hips made his cock look enormous even though he was just chubbed. A silver ring glinted from the tip.

The bear continued. "I want you to get close to him. Make him trust you. Fuck him if you have to. Let him fuck you if that's what it takes. After what I've put in the light, I won't have an uncontrolled variable at the top."

The light? Right, La Luce.

"Anything else, Giacomo? Just get close to him?"

Giacomo! The bear was Giacomo Barbieri, the investor, or as Alec called him, the cunt. He thought this guy was involved in stealing the client list.

The translation app closed in favor of Andretti's name in caps, along with his number. I managed not to curse aloud as I dismissed the call and swapped back to the app.

"Enough of this chatter. I have a meeting soon," said Giacomo.

Carmelo took his cue and moved from the bear's shoulders, stroking oil onto his own cock as he positioned behind. That had to be ten inches. Giacomo groaned, and his fingers clenched as the waiter filled him. Slow and gentle to start, the investor raised to his knees before long. Carmelo looked so small behind the bear, but he made him moan and pound his fists against the marble.

So much for starting the day with empty balls. I worked myself, watching Carmelo grip the grizzly's hips and slam into him. Each thrust made me wince, but that didn't stop me. Giacomo pushed to his palms, rolling his eyes to the distant ceiling.

"*Ci sono quasi*," he yelled in time with Carmelo, who sped up, dripping sweat from his forehead onto the bear's back.

Fucking hell. Carmelo was big, but it looked like Giacomo had a tree trunk flopping stiff with the waiter's rhythm in the shadows beneath him. I lost myself in the mesmerizing undulation and clapped a hand over my gasp when he growled, cumming hard across the marble. Carmelo grunted, pinching his eyes closed and slowing his movements. It was too much, and I joined them from my dark alcove in the corner, making my mess on the blue tile.

Carmelo pulled out and grabbed for the towel to wipe his dick. I never saw him grin or show any indication that he was enjoying it. This was a transaction. Giacomo didn't see it with his face buried against his hands, ass still propped in the air, trying to catch his breath.

I glanced back at my phone as Giacomo spoke.

"Start with what we discussed and come to me tonight," Giacomo grumbled into the stone floor.

Without a word, Carmelo left toward the changing room, towel in hand. As I watched his tight ass go, I wondered what these two, or just Giacomo, might want from me and decided that I'd play along as if I didn't know. Maybe I'd learn something to take back to Interpol Alec. The one thing I knew with any certainty was that Carmelo would not be fucking me with that beast. At least not without a relaxing night filled with liquor, poppers, and an ice pack for the next week.

I watched Giacomo while the moments ticked by. Sweat and humidity glistened from his hairy back and ass, which he finally lowered to the marble, smearing cum across his stomach as he did. Then, like a bull walrus rolling off his rock into the sea, the grizzly flipped into the water. He stood a second later, the surface reaching his navel, and shook out his short hair before sliding down the edge, spreading his arms to lean his back against the pool's lip.

There were still hours before I was supposed to meet Andretti, but I didn't want to spend the time hiding on the floor in a bathhouse. I wiped up my mess with the towel and silently pushed to my feet, eyeing the curtain to the changing room. As quickly as I dared, I padded out of the alcove. Giacomo's gentle snores gave me the courage to speed up, keeping to the dark edges of the bathhouse. I took a final breath of the rosewater and eucalyptus before slipping into the changing room. I waited there for a breath, listening for any signs of Carmelo, before peeking around the corner and seeing the empty locker room.

The sun blinded me after so long in the soothing darkness of the Turkish bath. Halfway back to my suite, I checked my phone and saw the seven missed calls from Andretti. Groaning, I called him back.

He answered immediately. "Where the fuck have you been?"

I held the phone away to recover from the outburst. "Hello to you, too."

"Lovely to be so flippant. Might I remind you that a man is dead, and we're hours from losing everything?"

I sighed out a long breath to collect myself. "Yes, of course. Are there any developments? Do you have Enzo?"

"Petras is questioning him now. He seems shaken and emotional, but it could all be an act."

"What do you need me to do?"

"You are the face of La Luce, Mister Demetriou. I need you available. Wait in your suite and answer your fucking phone when I call." He hung up.

Did I call him for him to yell at me to answer my phone? I imagined the spittle flying on his end and how red his cheeks must be. What a difference to the calm, wine-sipping, stick-up-his-ass lawyer.

The sun sizzled on my nose and arms while I stood in the path, debating what to do, but knowing there was only one option: do as Andretti bade me. We had to get through the next few weeks to the grand opening, and I wouldn't help that by wandering and exploring.

The other mystery of the ChatSphere contact nagged at me as I walked. They knew I'd overhear something of interest and put me in the best place to overhear it. Did that give me any clue to their identity? Maybe Santiago was feeding me information that he couldn't say publically? Eli using me as his ears?

The lobby was empty, save for a thin man in a tank top, board shorts, and sandals by the elevator. I recognized his gauged ears, undercut, and tattoos at the distance.

I should have expected this.

"Carmelo, good morning."

He turned to me with that flirty smile he'd flashed so many times in the restaurant. A smile absent while I watched him grunt into Giacomo a half hour ago. "Mister Demetriou. I was coming to see how you were settling in." His English was as soft as his Italian, if spoken slower.

"As well as I can. I assume you heard about Herr Jensen?"

"I just came from a meeting with Mister Romano," he nodded. "So sad. He was a kind man. And terrifying that something like that could happen here."

"I have a meeting in a few hours, but it looks like you're off the clock. Would you like to come up for a bit? I'm trying to get to know the staff." I took the elevator key from my pocket and pushed the call button.

"I wouldn't want to impose, Mister Demetriou," he said, yet joined me in the elevator car.

If the grizzly bear sent him to flirt with me, I'd give it right back. "Please, call me Matteo."

As the doors closed, all I could smell was rosewater and eucalyptus.

Twelve

Carmelo

"**C**AN I GET YOU something to drink?" I asked, stepping into my suite, relieved that breakfast was still on the table and my bed was a mess. No cleaning crews had slipped in while I was in the bathhouse.

"Tonic water, please," said Carmelo, crossing to the windows and folding his hands behind his head.

Did I have tonic water? I hadn't looked in the refrigerator except to see it stocked. Sure enough, there were three rows of it. Far more than I'd drink in a year, a lifetime. Actually, tonic water was the only thing to drink in the fridge. I grabbed one for each of us and joined him by the window.

"*Grazie.*" He uncapped the glass bottle and took a sip. "I've never been up here. It's strange to think about how it looked twenty years ago."

"How do you mean?"

He took another sip and shook his head. "It's nothing."

I leaned against the glass to face him, trying to see him without remembering his fingernails digging into Giacomo's hips. "I don't know much, or anything, about Isola di Luce before the resort. Tell me about it."

Carmelo ran a hand through his hair and scratched the back of his neck. "There's not much to say. Twenty years ago, we'd be looking over the village where I was born. There wasn't much to it. Lots of men fishing, women fixing nets. It hadn't changed with the times for a hundred years."

"You were born here? Lio laughed when I asked if he was. I wasn't sure why."

Carmelo scoffed. "Lio. He's one to be careful around, Matteo." He paused for another drink. I'd have to find a way to get him to tell me more about that opinion. "After the Italian government sold the island to your father for a lira, he started evacuating the village, resettling some in Xemxmarina and the rest to the mainland."

I hadn't heard any of this before. "Sold for a lira? Wouldn't that be like a fraction of a penny? Why?"

He leaned on the glass, facing me. "I assumed he had some leverage. Blackmail, or the like."

"Maybe he made them an offer they couldn't refuse." I waited for Carmelo to give a hint of recognition with my reference, but he gave none. "All the names are in Italian, but the village of Xemxmarina doesn't sound very Italian."

"You really do need a lesson about the island's history." He shrugged. "Gżira tal-Dawl was under Maltese rule for centuries. It changed ownership after World War II, when the Italian government took it over, renaming it to Isola di Luca."

I didn't know that simple fact, yet I was supposed to be the face of this place? "So, you were born here. Then what?"

"It was just my father and me. We were moved to Xemxmarina when I was eleven, but my father only fought against your father's work. We were evicted to the mainland a few months later."

"How did he fight against my father?"

"My father had strong opinions about a Greek man invading an island of Maltese who were given to the Italians two generations ago. He organized rallies and raised hell with the government trying to undo the transfer of ownership."

"Fair. I'm sorry about that." I took my first drink of tonic water, cringing at the bitter taste.

He shrugged; the sea beyond the buildings sparkled in his eyes. "You had nothing to do with it. My father passed a few years ago, suddenly and unexpectedly in his sleep, and I moved back."

"That's terrible. What happened?"

"They thought an aneurysm or stroke."

I wanted to pry more, ask if there was an autopsy, or if not, why not, but it felt like too much to ask when first sitting down with a man. "What made you want to move back?"

"The landscape is different, but the sunset is the same as I remember."

"You're a romantic."

"I'm a realist. My home village is gone, other than few roads and walls, and no amount of fighting will bring it back. I may as well enjoy what came from its destruction while I make a good living."

Fucking grim. If he was doing as Giacomo told him and was trying to get in my good graces, he was going for a sympathy approach. And it was working. I felt terrible for what he and his family had been through. What my father had put them through. Of course, that first ChatSphere message, warning me to trust no one, still stuck out. Carmelo might be creating a convincing fiction. It would be easy to ask around and learn the island's history before they broke ground on La Luce.

I beckoned for him to follow me to the door leading to the balcony, where I adjusted an umbrella to shade two chaises. I glanced around the pool below, not noticing anyone watching from the shadows this time.

"I've heard from a few people now about friction amongst the staff. Is there anything more there I should know about?"

Carmelo sat on the chaise, faced me, and pulled his feet up close, letting his knees drop open. I tried and failed to not notice the massive hump in his board shorts.

"I shouldn't have said anything about Lio," he said. "I don't want to color your opinions."

"I'll keep it between us." I sat on the chair's edge, knees close to Carmelo's.

He finished his tonic water and traced a finger around the ridges on the bottle's bottom. "He's always looking for an opportunity. He attached himself to Benedikt the moment he stepped foot on the island. Now he seems smitten with you, and poor Herr Jensen is dead." He touched the ankh resting on my chest.

I placed my hand over it as he pulled back. Yesterday, I told myself that I'd trust Lio. Now, the way Carmelo talked, I would have thought the same about him had he gotten to me first. Obviously, I couldn't really trust Carmelo, knowing he was here on Giacomo's bequest. I never would have guessed that by how openly he spoke.

"It sounds like you think he might be involved in Herr Jensen's death," I said.

He shook his head. "Benedikt was a powerful man on this island. If this were more than an accident, it would take a force of nature or passion beyond what I assume Lio is capable of."

"You don't think too highly of Lio, do you?"

He waggled a hand side to side. "We all have our thoughts about each other. Is it so bad a thing if someone thinks you're too soft to commit murder?"

Good point. "What about Enzo, his son? I only met him briefly, but he felt like a force of nature."

Carmelo frowned. "Can we talk about something else?"

"Yes, sorry. You're a waiter. Do you have any other roles at La Luce? Your hands look strong like you could be a baker, kneading dough all day." I waved my bottle at his hands fidgeting with his in his lap. If he suspected what I was trying to draw from him, he didn't give any tells.

He flexed his left hand and looked down at his palm. "We wear a lot of hats. Mister Romano has me in the restaurant, but that might all change when there are more guests after the grand opening."

"Any fun hobbies? Five-year goals?"

He smirked. "I love to surf, but the Mediterranean is not the best for that. Five years? I don't know. I'd like to be on the island still, but with a lower stress job than what I'm doing here."

Did he mean the stress of patrons snapping their fingers to demand their drink be refilled or joylessly servicing investors? "Let me know if you have another position in mind, and I'll see what I can do to move you toward it." Christ, I sounded like all the bosses I hated. "And maybe a company trip to Hawaii to ride the waves."

His smile widened, looking absolutely genuine. "What time was your meeting? Mister Andretti didn't sound like he wanted you to be late."

"One. I should get ready for that," I groaned. "Despite getting grim, it was nice to talk with you, Carmelo."

"It was for me too." He smiled and nodded down to the bottle of tonic water forgotten in my hand. "I suggest you develop a taste for that, Matteo. Your father drank nothing but it."

I choked down the rest of the bottle and rose to escort him to the elevator. My phone buzzed as the doors closed. Andretti. Who else would call me?

"Yeah?"

"Meet me... lob... med..." His connection was terrible, and he sounded rushed and winded.

"Say that again? Did you say the lobby?"

The call ended.

I checked the time: a bit past noon. The morning already felt like a full day. Had it only been fourteen or so hours ago that we had dinner? It felt like a lot more. I'd heard and seen a lot to expand my confusion regarding my place on the island and nothing to answer any questions.

I ran my tongue across my teeth, surprised by the clean aftertaste left behind by the tonic water. Its initial assault of bitterness was long gone, leaving only a lasting bit of crispness from the carbonation on my palate. Maybe it wasn't as bad as I remembered it being. That had probably been dollar store shit. La Luce would only stock the best of the best.

Thirteen

Lies

I WAS IN THE lobby in under two minutes, but Andretti was already there, pacing. His suit was rumpled as if he'd slept in it, but by the bags under his eyes, he looked like he hadn't slept in days. Quite the difference to how I'd seen him sipping wine at dinner last night. He'd been focused on the work, annoyed with how drunk Eli was getting. Now the lawyer looked ready to snap.

He raced to me, digging his fingers into my elbows, close enough for me to see the red veins in his eyes.

"I'll fucking kill him," he spat. "Slit his fucking throat and toss him out for the seagulls."

"Petras?" I tried to pull back, but his grip was iron.

"He let Enzo go, and now our only suspect is at large."

Andretti released me, and I rubbed my elbows. He was a lot stronger than he looked, or maybe the rage fueled him. "Enzo fled? That doesn't look good for him."

"I didn't say he fled. Petras released him, and he left. He can't get away. The island is still on lockdown from the—" He glanced around the empty lobby and lowered his voice, "from the other matter. We assume he went to his family estate in Xemxmarina, but the fact remains that we are hours from admitting to the investors that a murder has happened without surveillance, and the sole suspect is roaming the island."

"Did Petras interrogate Lio?" I sucked in a breath, as if that could pull the question back into my mouth.

"Who?"

"Lio..." Shit, Carmelo said Lio's last name in the bathhouse less than an hour ago... What was it? "Lio Carbone, a porter."

Andretti stared at me for a breath and shook his head. "Him, yes, of course. Petras held him after the staff meeting but chose not to hold him. Do you know something I should?"

"I'm sure I don't." I took Andretti's arm, pulling him toward the back doors. "How much of that do the investors need to know? Eli told the staff about Herr Jensen this morning, so we should assume everyone knows he's dead, if not the details."

Andretti narrowed his eyes. "Mister Romano did not tell the staff about what you discovered last night. I specifically instructed him not to and I sat in on the meeting. He called everyone about this little party for you in a few hours and a reminder about the investor meeting tomorrow. He told them the island is locked down, but not why. He wants everyone as attentive as possible. The meeting was unrelated to Herr Jensen's death."

But... Carmelo said... No... He never actually said Romano announced Jensen's death in the meeting, but he clearly already knew from some source.

I brushed it aside for the moment.

"Santiago suspected foul play. Why?"

"The garden rocks were raked hours before but tossed around with clear signs of a struggle."

"You're the lawyer, Andretti. Even with all my knowledge coming from American crime dramas, as you called them, some disturbed rocks aren't enough to jump to foul play. Herr Jensen might have had a heart attack, stumbled through the zen garden, and fell hard on a rock. It's unfortunate but conceivable. And it's a lot better than saying someone was murdered. I don't want to cover something up, but we gain nothing from jumping to the harsher conclusion."

Andretti stepped back, rubbing at his stubble and hiding his grin. "You are devious, Mister Demetriou." He tapped his upper lip. "This could work. Smoothing over Petras' oversight will be another matter."

"The cameras? La Luce is all about anonymity, yes? So why should there be cameras everywhere? The investors should see it as a boon that things can go unseen. If I were a republican senator from Louisiana coming to get my rocks off before going home to vote on a bill to criminalize what I just did, I wouldn't want any evidence I was here. The cameras being off is a good thing."

"Oddly specific, but not untrue. Yes, I have been looking at this from the wrong direction. This only leaves the stolen client list— the unrecovered list— which is again beyond the scope of what the investors must know." Andretti took a deep breath and smoothed his suit, seeming to notice his disheveled state for the first time. "We will make it clear their money is being properly managed, their returns are guaranteed, and skip to teasing them with plans for the opening gala. Thank you, Mister Demetriou. You talked me off the metaphorical ledge." He clapped a hand on my shoulder, squeezing it.

"Glad I could help," I said, looking down at his hand on me.

"I have underestimated you. You would have made a decent lawyer thinking like that. You will do alright here." He finally took his hand from me, brushing my shirt smooth as he did. "You remind me of your father, with quick thinking like that."

"I just want to come up with something feasible until we actually know something."

Andretti shook out his wrist to check his Rolex. "It's barely half past noon. I know I intended to brief you fully, but my time would be better spent ensuring a united message among all the managers. If Enzo approaches you, tell him what we have agreed upon and that we assume it was all an accident. Keep him in place and get a message to me."

"Why would Enzo come to me?"

Andretti sighed. "It pains me to say this, but there are factions among the staff and residents of Isola di Luce. Your father tried to stamp out such in-fighting until his final day, but it still exists. It is nothing you need to concern yourself with today, only to be aware of it. You represent an unknown, Mister Demetriou. You wield power and influence, and others will attempt to steer that or leech it from you."

"What faction is Enzo a member of?"

He shook his head and waved down my question. "Do not worry about that. Just keep him calm and talking, should he come to you, which I doubt he will. I will see you at the mixer."

Andretti turned to leave, passing Lio as he walked in. The lawyer gave the porter an obvious up-down, then back at me with a smug look before leaving the lobby with a loud sigh.

Seeing Lio was about the last thing I wanted at that moment, but I slapped on a smile all the same. He was back in uniform with his pink polo that struggled to contain his biceps and little blue shorts straining around his thighs. No, that was wrong to say I didn't want to see Lio. He was wonderful to look at. But right now, I wanted to hide away and spend time alone, scouring the internet for more of Carmelo's story. I'd act my part and be a good face for the resort until I could find a way to sell it out to enact global change.

"Hey, Lio. I see you found some clothes."

He didn't slow his pace until he slipped a hand around my waist and kissed my cheek. "Hello, Mister Matteo." He dropped his hand and stepped back. "You smell nice."

"Thank you. Andretti canceled our meeting, but I have some studying to do before the party. What are you up to this afternoon?"

Lio stared at me for a breath before blinking hard and shaking his head as if dismissing a stray thought. "I just came from settling Herr Albrecht and am delivering a package for him." He hefted the small box wrapped in brown parchment that I hadn't noticed in his hand until that moment. "I thought I'd come by on my way and see how you were doing."

I could have forgotten that Lio was employed here. Of course, he'd do some work now and then. "Fewer meetings with Andretti will always brighten my day. Who is Herr Albrecht?" I stopped myself from asking what he meant by "settling" after what Lio did to help me get settled yesterday. That was his business.

"Henrik Albrecht. He designed the water and power systems on the island."

"Is he one of the investors?"

"Yes. He has more money than god, but you would never guess by how he dresses."

"Did he only just get here? The island's locked down."

Lio hummed. "Mister Romano mentioned that in the meeting this morning, but do you know why?"

I shook my head and shrugged.

"Maybe it's related to Benedikt. No one may leave, but ships may arrive. Herr Albrecht just arrived on his sailing yacht."

The conversation lulled awkwardly, or at least I suddenly felt awkward. Maybe it was a touch of guilt for how far things had gone last night. Or an equal lack of guilt. "I should get to what I was doing, and you should get that package delivered."

Lio's shoulders drooped with my dismissal.

"Why don't you come by after if there's time? You could perform your valet duties," I said, tracing a finger down his ample forearm.

That perked him up.

Andretti said there were factions and implied I should take care not to alienate anyone seeking my favor. I still felt like a dick doing it.

"I won't be long," Lio said with a wink.

"Take your time. I'll probably be out until after four." I pinched his chin between my thumb and the knuckle of my index finger, pulling him forward for a gentle kiss.

I stepped back, and he stood there grinning, touching a finger to his lips. Despite all my mixed signals, I hadn't felt more clear-headed since arriving yesterday.

Maybe the tonic water was good for me.

Fourteen

Mingle

I KICKED MY SHOES off the moment I stepped on my suite's plush carpet, letting the nap push between my toes. My shirt came off after a few more steps toward the dining table. Despite the AC pumping in my room, the stress had me sweating bullets. I'd go through a lot of laundry living here.

Propping my feet on the table, I leaned back, scrolling through my phone. I could do a language lesson, or a couple. Italian and Greek would be important, but so would Maltese and Arabic. I couldn't learn all those at once. Most of the signage in La Luce was in Italian. Xemxmarina would be as well, after seventy years of Italian ownership, and I was sure I would have a need to spend time in the village. Plus, with Italian, I'd be able to understand some of what Lio moaned last night. That wouldn't be until the advanced lessons, though.

I'd intended to read what I could about the island's history but instead fell into a rabbit hole of beginner lessons, the app rewarding me with cheerful jingles when I repeated something correctly and epic crescendos every time I unlocked an achievement. Gamifying language lessons was a genius idea. My mother and the aunties either spoke in a heavy dialect, making the phrases nothing like I remembered them, or something in the thirty years between scrambled my memories.

I felt confident about how to ask where the bathroom was and how to introduce my grandmother Philis when I noticed the time. Hours had slipped away to the dopamine-inducing minigames and layers of unlocks, slowly sipping tonic water, hating it a little less with each swallow. Throwing on yet another new set of clothes, I checked myself in the bathroom mirror, splashed some water on my face and through my hair, and was out the door within a few minutes.

Now that Carmelo told me some of the resort's sordid past, I saw more of his village within the layout and construction of La Luce. Narrow, curved streets wide enough for a cart, but not a car, with buildings two or three stories high constructed with careful stonework. The paths all had a slow decline as I moved toward the Mediterranean Sea, now and then breaking for a few stairs to speed the progress. Within minutes, I saw a freshly painted sign for "Romano's Loft" and ducked into the alcove with only an elevator call button beside the wood-paneled doors. Music thumped down from somewhere a few stories above me, and I gave myself a quick silent moment in the shady vestibule. This was a mixer in my honor, for people to meet, or at least see, me. All eyes would be on me. I hadn't done anything special with my hair, and I looked down at my loose, button-up shirt and pants, wondering if they'd be enough. I'd have to get better about being important.

I stabbed the elevator call button, and a presence filled the space beside me.

"Fashionably late, are we?" Santiago asked, his shirt unbuttoned enough to display whorls of chest hair.

I'd checked my phone a dozen times on the way here. "I'm right on time."

The elevator opened with a ding and Santiago cracked a smile. "With Eli, he expects the party to start on time, but you better be there early or show up drunk. Come on." He waved me to go ahead of him into the elevator car, gesturing with a black glass pint bottle.

"What's that?"

"Homebrew vodka. We both make and trade bottles of it. Don't tell the boss." He winked and pushed the roof button. Santiago's focus dropped to his hands, fiddling with the bottle.

"You two seem pretty close."

He sniffed. "When you work this closely with others, it's impossible not to. You either love each other as brothers, or hate your job and leave. For the most part, the staff's worked out their issues with each other by now."

The doors opened to the roof covered with a patchwork quilt of brightly colored sails that provided shade to the high-top tables dotted across the space. Music, little more than a bass track, thumped from speakers hidden in the planters and mounted on the sail poles. Two dozen men ranging from early twenties to their seventies were settled into their cliques, everyone with a drink in hand. A shirtless bartender was currently topping off Eli's martini from a shaker. My entertainment manager saw me and nearly knocked the drink out of the bartender's hand, waving.

"Matteo Demetriou! There's my man of the hour!" Eli yelled. Eyes shifted, and I sensed conversations pivoting to comment about me.

If this man accomplished so much while always bombed, what would he be like sober?

I met him halfway, and he grabbed my shoulder with his free hand, pulling me in to kiss each cheek. Bleary-eyed, he kept an arm around me and turned to face the dappled crowd. "I've assembled the ton of La Luce. A few more of your upper staff management, the mayor of Xemxmarina, disguised Italian politicians, and no fewer than two winners of the FIFA World Cup from the last twenty years. All mixed in with others from our soft launch, which, all things considered, is going quite well."

"Even considering last night?" I asked.

Eli's hand slid to my elbow, gripping tightly. "I have a very nice buzz going on to keep me from thinking about that, so don't start, Matteo." His dour expression lightened when he noticed Santiago holding up his liquor bottle beside me. "You old son of a fuck. What've you got there?"

"Go mingle," Santiago said to me. "I'll be with you in a few to help with introductions." Holding the bottle between them, he and Eli slipped away toward the farthest table.

"What'll it be, boss?" asked the bartender, leaning toward me. I put him around Lio's age, with a trim waist and a chest that could do a hundred pushups without breaking a sweat.

"Old Fashioned

"Whatever you'd like." The way he nodded was the same as all the overt flirtations I'd received at every openly gay bar. Good job, bartender; men liked being flirted with. I knew plenty of straight men who admitted they found it flattering. The ones that didn't were just insecure. He pushed back the drink on a paper square a few seconds later. "I made it strong for you, hon." He looked me over, biting his lower lip, and was on to the next customer. Being ogled by every man I encountered here might get old, but it wasn't getting old yet.

Leaning against the bar, I scanned the crowd, searching for someone I knew, and found none. I searched for the retired soccer professionals. Not that I would recognize them or know their names. I had a bloody piece of paper hidden back in my room that listed everyone here, along with the few dozen more that would arrive over the next weeks. Watching them mingle in groups, slowly getting drunk early in the afternoon, I wondered how any one of them would react knowing someone threatened to expose them. For many, coming to a male-only resort was nothing. For just as many, it would ruin their careers, their lives.

I took my first sip and breathed out the bourbon's gentle burn. It wasn't as good as Carmelo had crafted, though I was sure it used all the same liquor and bitters. It just showed that the ingredients were wasted on someone of lesser skill.

"Matteo Demetriou, I've been wanting to meet you. You're taller than I guessed."

I looked down at a man to my side wearing flip-flops, board shorts, and a bright blue t-shirt with a QR code in the center. His huge sunglasses obscured half his face.

"That's me, Mister..." I said.

"Kenji, hey." He offered a hand to shake, and when I reached to take it, he changed it to a fist bump. He tossed back the rest of his drink, something clear in a highball glass, and shook it at the bartender. I couldn't quite tell his accent. It sounded like a mix of several. "So, you're the big dick around here."

I spat a mouthful of bourbon into my glass rather than spray it. "I guess so?"

Kenji ran a hand through his straight, black hair. "I get that. It's weird when someone else's work is suddenly yours. I've been there." He took his new drink from the bar, raising it to the tender. "Thanks, Babes." Then turned back to me. "And you, ta for now. We'll be seeing a lot of each other." With his dark lenses, I couldn't see where he was looking, but I felt his eyes all over me. Maybe it was my imagination.

"Wait," I called after him, and he spun back dramatically. "What does your shirt say?"

He rushed toward me, clapping a hand on my chest. "You're the first to ask! I've been here twenty minutes and nothing. Everyone must assume it's some tech... whatever. Scan it and find out." He hopped back, tugging at the bottom hem of his t-shirt with his free hand.

I pulled my phone from my pocket, aimed the camera at him, and the text overlaid the QR code on my screen.

"AVERAGE DICK ENERGY"

I looked back up at him, his excitement clear despite not seeing his eyes. "Don't even say it. I know, right?" He spun away, laughing.

I snorted once, which led to a rolling chuckle. It was stupid, so stupid, and exactly what I needed at that moment: something to give me a genuine laugh.

Andretti approached the bar, passing Kenji and giving the weird man a sidelong glance as he did.

"Mister Demetriou," he said in greeting and raised two fingers to the bartender. "Do be careful with that one. Mister Nakamura's checks have always cleared, as it were, but he is a lot to deal with."

"What does that mean?"

"Mister Nakamura?" Andretti accepted a glass of red wine and watched me for a breath. "Mister Demetriou, I had hoped you would have spent your time these last hours studying the materials I provided for you."

"You... What? You said you were going to send them, but I haven't gotten anything."

Andretti sighed loudly. "I would have had them left on your table with the daily cleaning, but since you rescinded the key, they are at the front desk. You must ask for mail and messages if you're expecting something."

"How was I supposed to know that?"

"Anyway, Mister Kenji Nakamura is one of our core investors with a tech empire worth a quarter trillion euros. He's also an erratic twenty-three-year-old playboy with multiple advanced degrees who can fluently speak every language he's encountered."

I almost spat out my drink a second time. "A quarter trillion at twenty-three? How?"

"His grandfather built the cash foundation through means beyond our scope of interest, then his parents channeled that into an empire spanning Asia and most of Europe. Half of your American-bought cell phone is chips made or designed by NakaTech."

"I've never even heard of NakaTech."

"Yet they wield wealth influence across the world."

"What about his parents?"

Andretti sighed. "What constitutes news in America? Hiroshi and Aiko Nakamura died three years ago in the highest-profile train derailment in over a century. It threw the Asian markets into complete chaos for months."

I hadn't heard any of this, but was that really surprising? Foreign news rarely made it to the front page at home.

Andretti heaved a deep breath, taking a long drink from his wine. "I will see that you are fed proper news sources. Meanwhile, do read the materials I directly provide for you." He left toward another group, never looking in my direction. He wasn't mad but definitely disappointed, and that was worse.

I waved for the bartender. "Is there a bathroom up here?"

"Yeah, hon. Around from the elevator."

I followed where he pointed and thanked him, excusing myself. Why? I didn't know. I didn't need to keep the staff updated on my movements, but Andretti's quiet scolding stung.

Past the elevator, a hallway with stucco walls and wide wooden slats by the ceiling let in plenty of fresh air and light. Two older men came around the corner, deep in their conversation, pausing just long enough to grin at me with their obvious up-down. I grinned back, continuing past them into the bathroom. I wasn't used to being the object of so many hard looks. This would take some getting used to.

The bathroom had a ballpark favorite, and the type of toilet fixture I hated the most: a trough. What masochist designed that? Why would men, drunk on swill beer at a baseball game, want to squeeze in, shoulder to shoulder, and let their piss comingle into a single drain? What was that weird kink? There were also two normal urinals under the low, slatted window and three handicap-sized stalls. I moved to a urinal, and though I didn't really need to pee, I unzipped and readied myself to try, focusing ahead out the window to the back half of the rooftop.

I'd have to provide more for La Luce, whatever that meant. It would start with reading the research provided and keeping myself informed. I'd learn the history and culture of Isola di Luce, and... I'd already forgotten what Carmelo said the original name was. Me, a data analyst from Minnesota, little more than a glorified warm body to do data entry, was suddenly tossed in with the wealthiest, smartest people in the world. Andretti mentioned Kenji's multiple degrees. I was struggling to understand Italian verb conjugation when that kid probably had room to learn Elvish, Klingon, and Simlish.

People were talking outside the window, drawing me back to the present.

A man grumbled in Italian, one I recognized. The Bear. Giacomo. A gentler, feminine voice replied. They were away from the party, talking in tones that dripped of conspiracy. I tucked my dick away and pulled out my phone for the translation app.

"Is this necessary?" asked a feminine voice. I hadn't seen a woman among the mingling guests. I hadn't seen a woman since I left on my connecting flight to the island. A feminine voice could mean anything, but assigning a gender made it easier for me to imaging the scene beyond the window.

"It wouldn't be if he'd just tell us," said Giacomo.

"I'm telling you the truth, Signor," said another man. My heart jumped to my throat with the pleading in his voice. "Please, you must believe me."

I craned to see through the window slats, hoping for a glimpse of the conversation. I could see a little of what I could only assume was Giacomo, by the pure bulk of the shape, but I'd have to twist the slats wider to see anything more.

"A piece of paper worth more than you'll make in your life goes missing and you don't know where it is?" asked Giacomo. "If that's how you are with security with all ten fingers, what's the harm in me breaking a few?"

The client list. Giacomo knew about it and wanted it, but that wasn't Agent Alec being threatened on the other side of the wall. This guy had a Spanish accent. I pinched the edge of a slat, daring to raise it a fraction of an inch.

The man was shoved against the window, rattling it, and I stumbled back. A dull thump, and he cried out, falling away. Giacomo probably punched him in the gut.

"Just tell him," said the woman, sounding almost bored as she spoke.

"I don't have it, I swear," said the man, close, sounding weak.

"Next time, Noah," said Giacomo, sounding close, "I won't be so nice. Keep the cameras off."

The man, Noah, moaned below the window as Giacomo and I assumed the woman, as well, left.

Keep the cameras off... Was IT's incompetence regarding the nonfunctional cameras intentional?

I rushed from the bathroom, down the hall, and past the elevator. The party had doubled in occupancy since I stepped away, or maybe it was just Giacomo taking up so much space. My general manager stood beside him, making Santiago look like an average-sized person. More waiters passed between the groups, offering premixed drinks and hors d'oeuvres. I picked out Carmelo on the far side by the bar.

The roof wrapped around the other side of the elevator, toward where I assumed Noah was slumped against the wall, holding his gut, worrying about internal bleeding. I didn't know the guy, but that didn't stop me from worrying about him.

"Mister Demetriou, come meet someone," Santiago's voice cut across the roof.

I froze, cursed, and plastered on a smile before turning toward the bear.

Santiago gave me the grin of someone who wanted to leave the party. "Mister Demetriou, let me introduce Signor Giacomo Barbieri, one of La Luce's premier investors."

Fuck. I knew he was an investor and part of the paperwork Andretti left at the desk by my elevator. "Signor Barbieri, a pleasure."

The bear shook my hand. I could maybe touch my fingertips around two of his digits. I thought I got a whiff of rosewater and eucalyptus from the bathhouse.

"*Non parla Italiano?*" he asked toward Santiago, who shook his head. Giacomo sighed and plastered on a smile. "I look forward to making a great deal of money together, Mister Demetriou. Things seem to be going well so far."

He had to be bluffing. He obviously was. He just beat the shit out of some guy around the corner. A few hours ago, he set Carmelo to spy on me, but I couldn't tell if the waiter was a double agent or just doing what he needed to stay afloat. Were triple agents a thing? What did Giacomo know about the client list or Herr Jensen's death? The cameras? How could I get away from this conversation and see to Noah?

Giacomo did the work for me. "I have a dozen things to attend to and have made my presence here. If you would excuse me..." He nodded to each of us and left for the elevator.

"We have some more requisite greetings," said Santiago, putting a hand on my shoulderblade. "Let's get through it so I can get home."

"I'll be fine mingling on my own. You can head out if you want."

Santiago grumbled. "Andretti made me promise I'd do this. Come on."

I glanced back toward the path around the other side of the elevators, close to the edge of the building, back toward where some stranger was huddled on the stucco roof, holding his guts. I could only hope that Giacomo's threats of future violence meant Noah would be well enough to seek help on his own.

Fifteen

Máti Mou

AFTER NEARLY THREE HOURS, after I'd met the last guest and off-duty staff member, and promptly forgotten most of their names, Santiago declared his work done. Eli joined us at some point, making an effort to memorize everyone's drink of choice. When Santiago finally left my side, I casually rushed around to the space behind the bathroom window. A metal staircase descended to the street below, but there was no sign of Noah.

Excuses made, I slipped away and wound my way through the streets toward my suite. My eyes shot down every corner and alley, hoping for a sign of Noah, wondering what I'd do if I caught the bear pinning another man against the wall.

I didn't see another soul. The guests were all at the party, and the staff were either there or enjoying a few hours while the boss was drunk.

"You have a package, sir," called the man behind the reception desk in my lobby in a Scottish accent.

I was about to take the thick, manila envelope, grin, and keep moving, but I forced myself to pause. I could forget all the names at the party, but I'd seen this ginger man behind the desk half the times I'd walked by.

"Thank you," I said, resting an arm on the counter. "We haven't been introduced yet; Mister—"

"Oh, I know who you are, sir," he grinned, his freckles burning a little brighter. "Cooper, sir."

"That's some accent you have, Cooper.

He managed to blush harder. "Aye, sir. Born and raised in Tobermory. Isola di Luce reminds me a bit of it if you squint. Xemxmarina, at least."

"Is that so?" I tapped the envelope on the counter. "You'll have to tell me more about it sometime. I should get moving. A pleasure to meet you, Cooper."

"You too, sir. Have a nice afternoon."

Once in the elevator, I chuckled, proud to have my first interaction that wasn't interweaved with lusty undertones.

Stepping out of my shoes and pulling off my shirt, as was quickly becoming my custom, I tossed Andretti's envelope onto the table with a thump and bent the brass tabs to open it. He no doubt expected me to commit it all to memory before Eli's party, but there had to be at least forty pages. I straightened them, folding back the creases, and flipped through them once, but only saw them as walls of text broken by tight tabular data and graphs. Up until last week, data like that was my job. Now, I found I wanted nothing to do with it after the slightest chance of escape.

With my stomach grumbling and head buzzing with bourbon, I dug through the freezer, found a bag of microwave chicken fried rice, and settled on the dining table with the lawyer's homework and a bottle of tonic water.

I skipped through the first few pages talking about the resort's power and water systems— I'd come back to that later— and stopped at one with a discretely taken photo of the grizzly himself, Giacomo Barbieri. He wore a suit that could probably be broken down into three garments for normal-sized men, and by the champagne flute in his hand and neat trim of his beard, I assumed this was snapped at some gala or fundraiser. The bottom half of the page described him.

> Name: Giacomo Barbieri
> Nationality: Italian
> Age: 58
> Background: Giacomo Barbieri hails from the rugged landscapes of Northern Italy, where he built his fortune in the construction and real estate sectors.
> Personality: Giacomo is known for his straightforward approach and disdain for unnecessary pleasantries. Known for his imposing presence and gruff demeanor, Giacomo is a self-made man who values hard work, loyalty, and family above all else. Despite his rough exterior, he possesses a keen business sense and a surprisingly generous heart, especially towards those he considers family or friends. Converse-

ly, those who act against his interests have been met with violence.

Investment Interest: Giacomo sees La Luce as a legacy project, a chance to create something enduring and significant. His interest is both personal and financial, as much of the resort's design and construction came from his plans to incorporate work from the existing architecture.

Criminal History: Giacomo had served over ten years across four prison sentences related to unsafe labor management, though his last term was in his early forties. The World Court views him as reformed.

Here it was in black and white: Giacomo Barbieri planned the demolition of Carmelo's home village. I had a few other details I could add about the man, like how he enjoyed getting his ass plowed by obscenely oversized dicks. What did he hold over Carmelo, though? Maybe he did something to allow Carmelo back on the island. I assumed his lack of recent prison sentencing meant he was smarter about his crimes. The man was still a criminal, just not getting caught by someone who would report him. It was interesting that a whole section was dedicated to criminal history.

I almost spat out my tonic water when I flipped to the next page and the picture of a slender woman in a form-fitting dress and wide hat. I knew nothing about fashion but sensed she embodied it here. It looked like she was at the same event as Giacomo's photo, and it might have been the grizzly's shadow on the left side of the frame.

Name: Vera Rossi

Nationality: Italian

Age: 53

Background: Born into Milan's elite, Vera transitioned from a celebrated ballet career to a shrewd businesswoman after her mother's death in the early 90s. Carefully riding the rise of technology and the internet, she has advised some of the richest men in the world.

Personality: Intelligent, intuitive, and diplomatic, Vera is a force in her own right. She balances her husband's intensity with a calm, strategic approach to business and life. Vera is deeply passionate about the arts and sees potential for cultural enrichment in every venture.

Investment Interest: Vera is drawn to the Isola di Luce's potential as a cultural and artistic haven. She envisions integrating the island's natural beauty into the resort, creating a unique destination that offers more than just luxury accommodations.

Criminal History: Seventeen counts of insider trading, fraud, and similar crimes. All cases were dismissed.

Well, I could tell these dossiers were written by a man, not being able to talk about a woman without referencing her husband. I wondered how he felt about her pouring money and resources into La

Luce, whoever he was. I shook my head, trying to dispel the train of thought.

Culture and arts on an island meant as a gay retreat? Did she not get the memo? Actually, that made perfect sense. As a stereotype, gay men loved the arts. I loved the arts. The clientele invited here would have thick wallets and zero second thoughts about purchasing any overpriced thing they thought would grant a moment's joy.

Was she the woman I'd heard with Giacomo as he beat up Noah?

The next page had a picture of a man in, I'd guess, his mid-forties on the beach. He held up a beer toward the camera, and his robe was open to show off his tight six-pack and loose shorts. His oversized sunglasses mostly obscured his face, but his hair was swept back and almost down to his shoulders.

Name: Henrik Albrecht
Nationality: German
Age: 51
Background: A visionary in renewable energy, Henrik's innovations have positioned him as a leader in sustainable technology. His commitment to environmental causes is more than just business; it's a personal crusade to effect global change.

Personality: Pragmatic, innovative, and slightly reserved, Henrik values efficiency and sustainability. He approaches problems with a logical mindset, seeking effective and environmentally responsible solutions.

Investment Interest: Henrik views the island as an ideal setting to test cutting-edge sustainable technologies. He believes the resort can set a new standard for eco-friendly luxury tourism and serve as a model for future developments worldwide.

Criminal History: Dozens of breach of contract complaints, but nothing that held up in court.

The next had a picture with a half dozen mostly naked men and two women on the bow of a yacht, but everyone was focused on the young man wearing a Speedo in the middle. I was starting to expect every wealthy person to have a physique that was somehow exceptional, but this guy was completely average. That somehow made him more real.

Name: Kenji Nakamura
Nationality: Japanese
Age: 23
Background: Heir to a vast family fortune built on successful ventures in technology and finance, Kenji has spent most of his life indulging in the luxuries that come with immense wealth. Educated at prestigious institutions in the Netherlands, Belgium, Denmark, and Japan, he holds an MBA from INSEAD, amongst others, but shows little interest in conventional career paths. Known for his extravagant lifestyle, Kenji is a regular at the most exclusive parties and events worldwide.

Personality: Charismatic, flamboyant, and somewhat impulsive, Kenji is a social butterfly with a penchant for thrill-seeking. Despite his carefree attitude, he possesses a sharp instinct for opportunities that promise both profit and excitement.

Investment Interest: Kenji sees the island resort as the ultimate playground for the wealthy elite, envisioning it as the premier destination for luxury and hedonism. He is particularly interested in developing high-end entertainment and nightlife options, including exclusive clubs, casinos, and event spaces that cater to affluent guests seeking unique experiences.

Criminal History: Arrested multiple times for minor offenses, such as public intoxication, nudity, and disorderly conduct, but never convicted. His family's influence and wealth have kept his record mostly clean.

Twenty-three with an MBA from France, impressive. The description referred to him as an heir with no mention of his parents' passing three years ago, and only specifically listed one degree. It also didn't mention him being a polyglot. What else was missing from the other three dossiers?

I flipped through the rest of the pages, but there were just the four dossiers. Four investors funded all of La Luce? Or, maybe these were just the top ones. A bruiser, a femme fatal, a tech nerd, and a party boy. Herr Jensen had been an investor, but could a tailor working out a tiny island in the middle of the Mediterranean possess the resources on par with the rest? The other pages were reports with line graphs and pie charts just like what I generated and stared at all day at my former job. The final had a handwritten username and password. "Updated" was scrawled across the top. At least Petras had done enough to reset my login info after the break-in.

Feeling like the investor details were not meant to be shared, I stuffed the dossiers back into the envelope and went to the small safe I'd found tucked in the corner of the mirrored closets leading to the bathroom. I'd trust these to the safe, but not the client list, apparently. That was still tucked in my dresser drawer.

Since I was thinking about the client list...

I booted up the computer in the closet and keyed in the credentials from the note. The operating system was nothing I was familiar with, with the left side of the screen dominated by a sort of command prompt with green text on a black background updated regularly, but it all meant nothing to me. Whatever words that were on the screen were in Italian. I clicked on a few of the icons, bringing up more screens asking for logins, but my password didn't work on any of them.

The last icon was for tomatimou.mp4. Was that "toma timou"? "To mati mou"? "To Mati"? I went by Matty through college. Could this...? No, it was silly to think a twenty-year-old nickname would be misspelled in a file here. Though, my ChatSphere profile was still MinnGreekMatty.

I clicked it.

The video viewer opened with a blurred still of the movie's first frame. I could kind of make out that it was a person silhouetted with a window behind them. An error message dinged, and I used my phone to translate the text on screen.

"This file is password encrypted. Would you like to proceed?"

I clicked accept.

"You have 2 of 5 attempts remaining. This file will become unrecoverable upon failure."

Three attempts already used? It must have been the asshole that broke in to steal the client list. When would Agent Alec get back to me?

I clicked continue, and another dialog box replaced the warning with "My only regret" written in English above a text box and submit button.

No wonder the hacker failed to open the file. It's hard to guess such a personal answer when you don't know whose question it was.

Well, no. This was my father's suite up until a year ago. I shuddered at the thought that it had been his bed, his shower, his balcony... His bottle of lube... I hadn't thought about my father in decades, now he was everywhere.

But that also meant this had been his computer, so it was probably his video and his security question. The fact that it was written in English could be a clue.

"What would you actually regret?" I asked the screen. "It wasn't leaving me or Ma alone in New York. It seems like you did everything you wanted to in La Luce, other than not dying, but you wouldn't have known that when you set a password. An unrequited love? Picking the wrong quarterback for your fantasy football team?"

I couldn't answer the question for a man I knew nothing about.

I had two guesses, though.

I didn't know the man, but found myself wishing he regretted not knowing me. The Italian government selling an inhabited island to him might imply a life of danger. What if he was forced to abandon my mother and me for our own safety? I was clutching for straws, but what if...

I typed "Matteo" into the box and slapped the submit button.

The error buzzed, warning me I was now on my last attempt. Of course, my father didn't regret anything about me; he barely knew me. Perhaps my mother? I typed "Sophia" but hesitated. My father couldn't have regretted anything with Matteo, because Matteo was a full-grown man who chose to use his full name, rather than the one everyone called him as a kid.

I deleted my mother's name, typed "Matty," and hit submit before I gave it too much thought.

The video file closed, and the computer hard drive whirled. Just as I was sure the file was forever scrapped from existence, the window reopened without the blurring effect. The man staring back at me had my ears, dark eyes, and a dimple on his right cheek, though his short-cropped hair was shot with white. This had to be Rafael Demetriou, my father. By the background, he was sitting at the dining table with the wall of windows behind him. The datestamp in the bottom right showed this was recorded less than three months before his death.

The video started playing on its own.

"I've seen these kinds of videos in countless dramas, and there's a strange thrill in recording one myself," my father began, his voice light despite the heavy Greek accent coloring his words. "If you're watching this, it means I'm no longer here. This message can only be played once, so pay close attention.

"If this is Marco, I've left something more personal for you, hidden in our special place. Oh, Marco, I'm so sorry. I'll never forget when I first saw you across the Den, recognizing your profound sadness and growing alongside your soul capable of greatness."

My father took a breath to compose himself, pressing the heel of his palm into his eye, leaving me with an awkward and familiar phrase. Had Lio said the same about me? Was that a local colloquialism?

"If anyone other than Andretti is watching, I trust you'll ensure he receives this message discreetly. He'll understand what I mean.

"To Petras or anyone from IT who might be eavesdropping, fuck you. Your incompetence was a significant setback. We could have been celebrating La Luce's opening five years ago if not for you *malákas*. Whatever leverage you thought you had over me is worthless now. I'm confident Andretti or Santiago will rectify this oversight promptly. Don't let the door hit you in the nuts on the way out."

He paused, tapping his chin thoughtfully. "And to the other managers, I have laid the groundwork for La Luce to thrive independently, ensuring your prosperity for many years. It's crucial that you work together harmoniously—yes, Benedikt and Enzo, this especially means you."

He chuckled softly, "I should have planned this better." Then, with a sigh, he leaned closer, his expression turning earnest. "Matty, my dearest son, I dare to hope it's you watching. *Lypámai máti mou*," he said in Greek. I recognized the last bit from the filename. "I regret nothing more than not being there for you, not bringing you to this beautiful place I've poured my heart into. If Marco has guided you here, you're already part of La Luce's future. It's hard to believe, I know, given my absence in your life, but I love you deeply. If you do not already, you will soon know why I had no choice in leaving you. My greatest hope is that La Luce will be more than a legacy; it will be a testament to my love for you, filling the void my absence has left."

He touched his fingers to his lips, then the camera and the video went black. The viewer closed, and the hard drive whirred.

Sixteen

USB

I STARED AT THE screen for minutes while the meaningless green numbers updated along the side. My mind alternated between thinking of absolutely nothing and "What the fuck?" Were my father and Andretti an item? What leverage did Petras and IT have over my father? Carmelo made it sound like the staff was divided into stark factions, not just a little disharmony. How fucking dare he miss out on everything about my life, then record his regrets from the other side of the planet.

Despite my rage, my fingers touched the screen where my father had been. I barely had any memories of him, seeing him more in the old photos stuffed in a shoebox under my mom's bed, and here he talked like he missed my little league game. Two paths diverged before me...

Trust that my father wanted to, but couldn't, contact me for decades and learn everything I could about him and his intentions left behind for me in La Luce.

Or go with my gut, say screw the old man, and carry on with my half-assed plots to sell out La Luce for political power sometime down the road.

No... If that were my gut, I wouldn't have gotten on a plane with Andretti to cross the Atlantic. I wanted to know about my father.

Great. Something else for the pile.

I couldn't figure out how to navigate the computer's operating system to shut it down, so I held the power button until the screen went black.

Thoughts of my father spun through the forefront of my mind, a rare place of honor for him. Andretti would be the key to learning anything.

I picked up my phone, debating if I should text the lawyer, and saw a new message in ChatSphere on the first thread.

> **+34 58 4115 7011: pooltime**

Could that be Agent Alec? I first saw him by the pool as I jerked off on my balcony. Maybe his solo "follow me" message sent outside Enzo's shop hit some server error and didn't group it with the others.

Maybe, maybe, maybe.

Do something.

I crossed to the balcony door. Hands on the wood railing, I squinted in the afternoon glare, scanning across the pool below. There, on a lounge chair, sat an innocent package wrapped in beige butcher paper, no larger than a ring box.

Fuck. That looks just indiscreet enough to be important.

Not bothering with a shirt, I took the elevator down to the pool. Four guests idled around the water, but none near the package. I felt a buzzing in the back of my head standing at the edge of the shade beside a tiki bar, eyeing the little package on a chair. Someone could be watching from any of the shadows, behind any bush, out any of the tinted windows of the rooms overlooking the pool.

No point in delaying. With my head high, looking like one who belongs where he was, I strode to the chair, picked up the light box, and was back in the shadows a few seconds later. Another two minutes and the doors were opening into my suite while I rubbed a thumb on the box's course paper.

I tossed it where I had Andretti's dossiers and paced behind the chair. Maybe I should take this to Andretti right away. Though, I should open it first. What if it's an airborne poison? What if I need to just shut up and do something?

Snatching up the box, I ripped the perfectly cut piece of tape on the bottom. Underneath the crisp folders of the rough paper, the flat bottom and rounded top felt like a ring box. I tore off the paper and opened the hinge.

A USB drive, less than an inch long, sat on top with yesterday's date written across it with a felt pen.

Back to the computer.

After logging in again, I shoved the drive into a slot on the side of the monitor, and a familiar-looking window opened on its own, showing a list of folders with serial numbers for names. I scrolled through, opening a few at random, each full of video files named with a datetime stamp. Clicking a few of those, I saw they were camera feeds from around the island. The street with Herr Jensen's tailor shop, a pool, another pool, the front lobby just under my suite. Cooper stood behind the desk, dancing in place to something the feed didn't pick up.

Two videos sat alone at the end of the folder list, and I clicked the first one.

I recognized myself from what I'd worn to dinner last night, walking up the left side of the frame. The raked stones ringed with jasmine... This was the zen garden. This was footage Andretti said didn't exist. I would have thought the image froze, but the timer kept ticking by, so I skipped ahead until something changed.

20:41, two people came into frame on the left. By his trimmed gray beard, I guessed one was Herr Jensen, but the other kept obscured by features of the zen garden. They were agitated, both gesticulating wildly. Jensen kept trying to touch the other, but he was pushed away. They paused as another approached from the other direction. Wild, dark hair. Enzo. The three were gesturing, a fight was heating up. The hidden man landed a hook across Enzo's jaw. His father tried to pull them apart, and tripped backward. I winced at how the man's head bounced against the rocks. They dropped to inspect him, and a minute later, the two figures fled in opposite directions at 20:48.

Herr Jensen lay motionless in the rocks.

I fast-forwarded, and the video quickly lost light until it snapped into infrared, and I walked in from the other direction. I slid to the rocks, calling for help.

"Good to know he wasn't murdered," I mumbled.

The other man kept his face turned from the camera, but I didn't need to see it. From his thick build, dark hair, and pink shirt, I had an idea, but not one I wanted to give voice to.

The second video's file size was much smaller, showing the lobby below. Cooper wasn't at his post. 20:28, the elevator doors opened, and Lio exited, pulling on a pink shirt as he walked to the exit. The video cut to 20:57 and Lio, wearing only his blue shorts, jogged to the elevator, frantically stabbing the call button. He fell in as soon as the door opened.

I stared at the video's last frame frozen on the screen, of the elevator doors mostly closed.

The world pulled in at the edges. Lio swore up and down, seemed shocked when I told him the news, but I hadn't explicitly seen his right hand last night, plus I was exhausted. I'm sure the knuckles would have been red from that hit. Andretti hadn't mentioned anything about Enzo having a black eye or broken jaw. Though...

I'd fucked a killer last night.

No, no... The video clearly looked like an accident. I'd fucked a manslaughterer.

I'd watched a man die on film, a body I'd discovered, and confirmed the man I'd slept with was involved and lied about it. Yet I was grinning.

I had an answer. We wouldn't have to lie to the investors tomorrow, or at least we could make up a better fiction, knowing the truth. I didn't know who supplied this footage, which Andretti said didn't exist, leading to more questions, but at least I knew this one thing.

Herr Benedikt Jensen was not murdered.

Not exactly.

My fingertips slid across the screen, over that frozen frame of Lio in his blue shorts in the elevator, and the ankh's chain burned into my neck.

I ripped it off, gripped fingers through my hair, and slammed a fist against the computer's sturdy frame.

Fucking hell, this sucked. Lio showed every other sign of being worthy of my trust, yet, there he was, plain as could be. Whoever sent the video edited the clip to ensure I saw what they wanted me to see: That Lio could lie to my face, put on a great act, and make me want more from him. I was clearly not the great judge of character I never claimed to be. I only wanted Lio because of his muscles and apparent desire for me. His desire was probably little more than latching on to someone who could take care of him.

The video was edited... Could it have been doctored to point a finger at Lio? Spliced from old footage and smoothed over using AI? Was I grasping at straws for anything to disprove the obvious, that Lio had been present and involved in Herr Jensen's death?

Despite everything, I'd have a hard time refusing him when next he called on me. Until then, I caught a whiff of what the surge of stress and adrenaline did to my body and stripped for a quick, cold shower.

Seventeen

Cabana 9

S ITTING AT MY KITCHEN island, with my hair still wet from my shower, I had the client list set in front of me and idly spun the USB drive on it. Everyone had warned to watch out for those lying to me, but the opposite list would be shorter.

Lio told me some shit about him being my lighthouse but look where that got my father. He jumped or was pushed from one. I knew it was a mix of metaphor and reality, but the effect was the same. There was no one worthy of my trust on this island. Everyone had their layers of agendas. Maybe Andretti, but he only spoonfed me what I needed to know at that instant. Any information needed to be verified and vetted, however that might happen. Even if I was working with Interpol Alec to take down Barbieri or with Andretti to keep the investors' trust, I was on my own.

This called for a list with columns and bullet points. There would be paper with the printer in the closet, if anywhere, but my phone dinged as I rose to get it.

A new ChatSphere message. Before this trip, I hadn't opened this app in years; now, it's all anyone used to communicate. It was my dear friend, Nameless Spain Extension.

> +34 58 4115 7011: 7pm, Cabana 9

> MinnGreekMatty: Stop ordering me around. Who are you?

> +34 58 4115 7011: I'll tell you when it's safe.

I'd met Agent Alec there yesterday; it must be him. The time was less than forty minutes away, so I folded the client list around the USB drive and shoved them into the pants in a dresser drawer. Nowhere in my suite was safe, but I felt a little comfort in the security through obscurity.

Dressed down to a linen shirt, shorts, and deck shoes, I arrived at the cabana a few minutes early. My confidence about who I was to meet waned when I noted Alec and I first spoke in cabana seven. Right on the hour, a shadow flicked across the sheer curtains, and Enzo Jensen stepped into the cabana's opening. He'd styled his wild, curly hair down to hide some of the swelling on the left side of his face, but a blind man could see his black eye.

"Matteo!" He jumped back a step, eyes flicking across the small space as if to ensure I was alone.

"Who did you expect?"

"I'm not sure. I didn't think you were one to send cryptic messages."

Enzo glanced down at the cell phone in his fist, tapped the screen a few times with his thumb, then tucked it away in his back pocket.

"On ChatSphere?" I asked.

"Chat what? No, just a text."

"What did yours say?"

Enzo huffed and pulled out his phone, stabbing the screen and flashing me a chat from "Unknown" with the same "7pm, Cabana 9" text. A full screen of Enzo's responses followed it, demanding to know more, each with more capitalized letters and punctuation than the previous.

"I got the same. Who sent it?"

He shoved his phone away. "I'm sorry. Did you see a response that I missed? I figured I'd find out when I got here, but if it wasn't you, then I don't know."

A third party wanted us to meet, but why? Was this another situation like the bathhouse, where we'd be privy to something else by being in the right place? I figured I might as well get some conversation going.

"I'm sorry about your father."

"Thanks." His voice lilted up almost like a question, and he put his phone away again. "It doesn't feel real, you know? Like it hasn't hit me yet. Our parents usually, hopefully, don't outlive us, but I expected he'd get blood cancer or the like. Something I'd see coming."

My father saw his death coming with enough time to decide to step out early, yet he never thought to contact me. He looked fine enough in the video recorded three months before his death. I thought ALS took years to progress.

Though I knew the answer, I wanted to know what Enzo would say. "What happened to your eye?" My voice dripped with concern. I could be a good actor when needed.

He raised a hand to cover the shiner. "The porter, Lio, did this. Guy's a fucking maniac."

My fingers went to where the ankh had rested, and I was grateful to have taken it off in my suite. Didn't Enzo have some reaction to seeing it yesterday? Though, if his father had one as well, did Enzo think I got it from him? "What were you fighting about?"

Enzo opened his mouth to respond but snapped it shut, narrowing his eyes to consider me. "You're really not going to ask me if I killed him?"

I laughed at the forthrightness and stopped myself with a hand clapped over my mouth. "Sorry! I didn't think you'd be so blunt."

He raised an eyebrow, waiting for me to continue.

"From what I've heard, you and your father didn't get along, but it's a far leap to murder."

Enzo tapped his chin. "You could be a politician with a non-answer like that. This place is chaos, Matteo. Petras was screaming at me that he knows I did it, says he has proof, but won't show me anything. It's all a scare tactic to get me to say I did something I didn't do. If he had any footage, he'd know what really happened."

I never claimed to be a detective, but I'd only ever know the truths if I caught people in their lies. "He won't, or can't?"

Enzo's eyes narrowed, and he tilted his head.

"I hear Petras fucked up, and none of the cameras were on," I said. Enzo might be a great actor, but I believed his wave of relief and annoyance. "What really happened? What were you and Lio fighting about?"

"The usual. How often he lost or ruined uniforms, his slow delivery times. The same old story. For the last year, it's been about how he broke my dad's heart after a year of them fucking."

"Herr Jensen didn't want his thing with Lio to end?"

"Would you?" Enzo scoffed. "Don't answer that. I've seen him naked, I know he's hot with abs and a killer dick. He's exactly my old man's type. I think Lio got a little too comfortable here, wanted to go off on his own, and broke things off to free up his schedule."

"Why have you seen Lio naked?" The question spilled from me before I knew why I cared.

Enzo snorted. "I walked in on him and my old man more than I care to recount. I dare you to try unseeing *your* father sitting in a corner touching himself while a man younger than you was on all fours scrubbing the floor, wearing only knee-high athletic socks. The image sticks."

I cringed. "Sorry, I shouldn't have asked. That's a long jump to murder, though," I said. "What do you think really happened last night?"

"Oh, I can do more than think. I saw it. I was there. Coming back from dinner, I found Lio and my father arguing by the zen garden. It was getting heated, so I stepped in, taking my father's side for once. Lio decked me. My old man tried to help, but Lio shoved and tripped him into the rocks. Fucking hell, Matteo. The sound..." His eyes glazed with the memory but not with the emotion of someone describing their father's violent death. "We both knew what had happened, that there was no point in helping him. Lio grabbed me, said if I said anything, he'd kill me next. He had murder in his eyes. I believed him."

The video didn't have sound, but everything Enzo said could match what I'd seen. I didn't see Lio grab Enzo, and the tripping and shoving might be an embellishment, but if Enzo was willing to admit being in the scene, even without knowing there was a video confirming it, it gave some credibility to the rest of his story. Lio flat-out said he never left my suite. How could I get him to amend his story without coming across like an accusation, where he'd shut down? Why was this my job?

Whoever gave me the video thought I could do something with it, but I wasn't beholden to some masked man sending anonymous messages and leaving packages by the pool.

"Did you tell Petras all this?"

Enzo snorted. "No, fuck him. I don't talk to cops. He was never interested in hearing what I had to say; he just wanted me to sign a confession. What now?" he asked. "Not to sound overly callous, but life goes on, at least for most of us. You still need your

fitting, though your clothes are already mostly fine."
He leaned back, eyes running over me.

"Right after I found your father's body," I started, bringing him back, "everyone was immediately
suspicious of you, Enzo. Everyone seems to know
about the problems between you and your father.
No, I don't think you killed your father, but others
do. Andretti thinks you should be in custody. Help
me understand why you don't have a motive."

Enzo sighed. "I have a goddamn lot of motive,
that's the problem. We fought over everything. De-
signs, fabric choices, finances. I publicly said more
times than that I'd be glad when he's dead, and I can
run the business how I want. I didn't mean it. I was
just being, I don't know, dramatic."

"Why didn't you just leave the island? Or start a
competing store?"

Enzo's gaze drifted past my ear. "While we were
at each other's throats, we thrived off it. I'm sure
we both did, or he would have kicked me out. He
dragged me back fifty years so I could appreciate style and quality while I forced him forward
to keep the business viable. Our loathing was how
we showed love." He sucked in a quick breath and
turned to the water, wiping a palm across his cheek.

I put a hand on his shoulder but had no words.

"He tried to help me, tried to stop Lio from hitting
me, and was killed for it. Lio killed him."

My arm shook with Enzo's quiet sobs. It wasn't
true. Lio didn't kill Benedikt. At least, I don't think
so from what I'd seen on the video. A blurry video
shot from a distance with no audio. How much was

it just me wanting Lio to be innocent, and this all a tragedy and big misunderstanding? Enzo was right on one thing about Lio: he had great abs and a killer dick. How great would it be if he actually wanted me, not for whatever perceived position of power I had on the island? Also, if he wasn't a murderer. Though there was no denying he was a liar, maybe he'd say he was trying to protect me or some chivalrous bullshit. He seemed to get off performing service; maybe this was an extension of that.

Enzo shrugged out of my touch, turning. "We should start a club, you and I. The Fraternity of Murdered Papas." He wiped at his nose and grinned. "We can workshop the name."

"Santiago said my father's death was suicide."

"And you believe him?"

Andretti had jumped right in to corroborate Santiago's statement, but so what? He'd been unemotional, practiced in how he said my father's body was never found, but I assumed that was the lawyer in him. What if it was more? What if he was robotically repeating the coverup? The first mystery ChatSphere message yesterday agreed with Enzo.

I shook my head. "I have to believe someone, but everyone contradicts each other."

Enzo crossed his arms, leaning against the cabana's support. "Fair. Consider motives: why are people nice? Lio wants to be your fuckboy, and you provide for him. The managers need a Demetriou on the paperwork. I'm sure you inherited more than the resort and a ton of money. Think about who would control your father's political connections. There are plenty of patriarchal systems across Europe and northern Africa that would uphold in you the promises they made to your old man. That means you've assumed your father's debt, too, so watch out there."

"And you? What are your motives?"

"Me?" He ran a hand through his wild hair. "I'm not trying to get anything from you. We're business partners now but we don't have to go beyond that. I've worked with plenty of people I don't even like."

Such as his father. "Andretti made it sound like you're on the run. He wasn't happy with Petras after he released you after questioning."

Enzo huffed, rolling his eyes. "Those two need to fuck and get over it. You don't bitch for years about someone sucking at their job and not fire them unless you're hoping to get something."

"Or have something on them."

Enzo cocked his head, smirking. "Blackmail? It sounds like you know something I don't, Matteo. You're a sneaky bitch after only a day here."

I was saved from answering by a blaring alarm and a whiff of smoke on the breeze.

Eyes wide, Enzo took off in a sprint toward the thin smudge trailing from a nearby building. The one I'd just left when I came to the beach yesterday.

The tailor shop.

Eighteen

Feuer

I WAS ONLY SECONDS behind Enzo with the alarms echoing around me, repeated to carry across the resort. Mixed with it were shouted cries, but I knew there wouldn't be a fire brigade. Maybe the village had something, but the shop would be smoldering coals by the time they got here.

I rounded the last corner to see the back of Jensen-Klassiker. Oily smoke curled from a back window but without the aggression of an accompanied inferno. Enzo threw open the back door, dashing inside with his shirt pulled over his nose. I paused, lacking the courage or stupidity to follow him in. Water poured from the overhead sprinklers, dousing everything in the shop. Craning my neck to see into the darkness, my mind spun with suspects but came up with only one.

Lio.

I easily imagined him smashing the back window with a rock, followed by a Molotov cocktail. As the only one who might implicate him in the murder of Herr Jensen, Lio wanted Enzo off the island.

Except, the back window was cracked to let in a breeze, not smashed by a rock.

A golf cart swung around the far corner, stopping just short of me. Andretti jumped from the passenger seat.

"What's happening?" he gasped.

"We saw the smoke and rushed here. Enzo's inside."

The driver stepped beside me, pushing his sunglasses up to keep his hair back while he dabbed at his brow with a handkerchief. He glanced at me briefly, his eyes so dark they might have been solid black, then spoke to Andretti in Greek. I heard Enzo's name.

"English, Petras," said Andretti.

Petras. I don't know what I expected from the man, but not this. A perfectly shaped beard, tanned and trim, and those eyes... I expected an incompetent oaf, not a model. But then, every man on his island was like him. I wouldn't have been surprised to learn I'd watched a few of his videos when I found a spare moment alone. Well, not watched, just skipped to the good parts...

The head of security hitched up his belt laden with a walkie-talkie, a can that was likely mace, and a few smaller pouches. "Enzo is inside?" he asked. He'd said a lot more when I couldn't understand him.

"Yes, he—"

Enzo staggered out, and I caught him by the shoulders, leading him a few steps away.

"Here's the murderer turned arsonist now," said Petras.

"Fuck you," Enzo said and fell into a coughing fit.

"What happened, Enzo?" I asked.

He shoved out of my hold. "Turn off the fucking water, Petras. It's ruining everything." Enzo shoved a finger into Petras' chest. They switched their argument to Greek.

Andretti sidled up beside me. "Why were you with Mister Jensen?"

"We're thinking about starting a boy band."

Andretti only stared at my attempt at sarcasm.

"There's a goddamn fire, Andretti!" I waved at the smoke still issuing from the open door and window. It had noticeably lessened.

"Mister Demetriou, La Luce is only weeks from opening, and shit is coming out of nowhere to hit the fan. A man may have been murdered, and you were with the most likely suspect. Now his shop is on fire." He spread his arms, palms up, imploring me for answers. "You could barely estimate the stress I am under keeping this from the investors, much less from the guests wandering the resort."

"I'm sure Petras has gotten everything running since the reaming you gave him this morning. Just go back through the footage."

Enzo yelled a curse, throwing his hands up at Petras. The security officer turned from him, speaking into the walkie-talkie. Enzo stormed over to Andretti and me.

"This was arson," he spat. "An iron burned through a stack of staff uniforms. You find out who did this, or I walk. As much as you need the Demetriou name, you need a Jensen just as much."

Andretti took a deep breath for his lawyer response, but Enzo cut him off. "Fix this, Andretti. Fix this now, or everything falls to shit. More than it already is." He turned on a heel, shouldering Petras as he passed him toward the main resort building.

The commotion had attracted two staff members in pink and blue. They moved with smiles, waving to the five guests coming to investigate.

Andretti ran a palm over his bald head, looking up at the faint smoke escaping the tailor shop. "I can have a repair crew here tomorrow, but the shop's stock is likely destroyed between the smoke and water." I wasn't sure if he was speaking to me.

"Funny, well not funny, but that a death will be easier to keep quiet than a fire," I said, watching the staff usher the last guest around a corner, out of sight. "What'll you tell the rest? That Enzo forgot and left an iron on? People might believe it, thinking he's lost to his grief."

Andretti chuckled. "I would have hated having you across from me in my court days, Mister Demetriou."

He started to turn away toward the shop, but I pulled him back with a fistful of his blazer's shoulder. "These lies stop now, Andretti."

He stepped a little nearer, his chest swelling. "You've only just arrived, Mister Demetriou. You have no loyalties, only seeing La Luce as a paycheck.

It is, was, your father's life's work... My life's work and I will not see it fail in the eleventh hour, no matter the cost."

He wasn't strictly wrong, but it was hardly my fault. I'd barely been on the island a day and it wasn't exactly easy to make friends and forge alliances when literally everyone was wrapped to their eyeballs in lies. He was kind of right about me seeing La Luce as a paycheck. My bank account had more money than I could spend, thanks to my father's work. That money was mine, even if I left in the morning, though.

"Stay in your lane, and do not make this more difficult for me or anyone else," said Andretti.

I choked back the "yes, sir" that almost passed my lips and glowered at him instead.

"Now," he said, smoothing his jacket where I'd creased it. "We just have to get through the opening, and you can return to the shadows if you choose. But tell me: why were you with Enzo?"

I wanted to lie or tell him it was none of his business, but how would that help me? If I could trick him into exposing himself in a lie, so what? As far as I could tell, I might own La Luce on paper, but Andretti pulled all the strings.

I'd tell him some, but I wasn't ready to mention the USB drive yet. If I gave up everything I knew, I'd feel powerless here. "Enzo wanted to know what I knew about his father's death. He wanted to tell me he was innocent and hoped I believed him."

"And do you?"

I nodded. "Enzo and Benedikt had a strained, unusual relationship, but I believe there was love in it. Any involvement was accidental."

Andretti scoffed. "Says the man with no basis for an opinion." He waved me off to approach Petras. "Status?"

The head of security spoke in slow Greek while motioning high up on the buildings. I followed where he pointed and could just make out the small camera mounted there.

Andretti ran both hands over his skull. "I swear to Christ, Petras. What have you been doing with all the funds allocated to you?" He held up a palm to stop the answer and turned to me. "Mister Petras says the cameras here are also not turned on. IT has been applying critical security patches for over a week, when it should have taken an afternoon."

Petras started again in Greek, but Andretti spoke over him. "I am uninterested in your excuses. It will be my ass in the crosshairs after Signor Barbieri finds out about the fire."

"Only him? Not the other investors?" I asked.

"His early work developing the resort's infrastructure makes him feel more entitled than the rest."

It took no effort to imagine Giacomo threatening the locals of Carmelo's village, and I was pretty sure that was as close to reality as the grizzly providing construction resources.

"Andretti, remind me why Petras is still here?" I asked.

"It is complicated. Your father required him to stay."

Petras blackmailed my father, but according to his video, that no longer applied. I set my shoulders, ready to make my first big decision in La Luce.

"Petras, who is your second in command?" I asked.

"Kostas," he sneered.

"Great. Call him here."

"He is already on his way." Petras waggled the walkie-talkie.

"Great, you're..." The declaration hung in my throat. Everyone seemed to agree the security manager was a waste of oxygen, but would it cause a larger crisis to sack him at the very end? What damage could he cause without a coordinated effort to remove him and his access? Until we knew who printed the client list, no one should be leaving the island, and someone with Petras' level of intimate knowledge about the resort shouldn't be left free and unemployed.

Petras was glaring at me, awaiting my next words. Andretti was casting me a sidelong look. I cleared my throat. "You're free to go back to your duties. Everything seems taken care of here. The sprinkler system did its job, and the fire didn't spread. Please prioritize the system updates so the security systems can be fully online."

His eyes narrowed, but he took a deep breath and nodded. Turning, he clipped the walkie-talkie on his belt, returning to the golf cart.

"I'll walk, thank you," Andretti mumbled as the golf cart sped away. He raised his hand and voice to address the new crowd of onlooking staff in their pink polos and little blue shorts. "Back to work, everyone.

Mister Romano will update you all tomorrow morning." My head clouded at watching them stride away, talking in clumps. A dozen extremely attractive men that, as Lio told me when I first arrived, serve at my pleasure. As I'd told Carmelo and Cooper, I should get to know each of them...

I staggered back when Andretti filled my vision. "Petras is incompetent, but leave his firing to me. I cannot express the danger he could pose to the resort if things are not handled in the correct order."

"That's why I stopped myself." I glanced over his shoulder at the last of the staff wandering off, and back to the lawyer, lowering my voice. "I know about what Petras had over my father, and it's no longer an issue."

He searched my face for the bluff, eyes narrowing and lips parting.

Maybe I should have been a goddamn actor.

"I'll not ask how you know about that or how you can say it's resolved. Not right now. You seem to have a way of slinking around." He shifted back, crossing his arms and shaking his wrist to check his watch. "Christ, it's late. Tomorrow will be a better day."

"It couldn't be much worse. How much longer can we keep the island on lockdown? The staff are starting to notice and question."

"We have no leads." Andretti sighed to the sky. "I told the investors a fiction. The shots fired were against the suspect with the client list, but they fled. No one was hit and the list is unrecovered. We may be forced to let the matter go, hoping the suspect comes to us with demands before going to the press."

If no one was hit, who was recovering in Xemxmarina with Alec's partner?

"Who told you all this?" I asked.

Andretti's eyes narrowed further. "Petras."

"And you believe him?"

"No, but I feel compelled to, without other evidence."

"What if I told you I already knew all of that due to my slinking skills?" I asked.

Andretti covered his grin, but I saw it in the creases around his eyes. "I would be impressed. Has your slinking accumulated any evidence?"

Had it? I had the list, but Andretti punched holes in Alec's story without having heard it. I wasn't ready to mention Interpol to the lawyer without first talking to the agent. Andretti could make more sense of my father's video, but that was one line about Petras' blackmail and a lot of personal baggage directed at me.

"Maybe, but nothing that would hold up in court." I cleared my throat. "Have Santiago lift the lockdown in the morning and put Petras on the first boat. Don't tell him he's shitcanned until he's almost to the mainland. Hopefully, Kostas will do a better job."

"Consider it done. The extra hours will give me time to schedule his off-boarding. We're far from in the clear, Mister Demetriou, but you seem to be working out well. Keep your brunch open tomorrow." He tugged at his jacket, straightening the lines. Taking his cell phone from an inner pocket, he dialed as he turned away, speaking in rapid Italian. Maybe the repair crew, but I didn't care. Andretti seemed considerate enough to keep the conversation around me in English, so this was him doing something that didn't involve me.

Enzo said Lio grabbed and threatened him, but that wasn't on the video. Maybe his memory went a little off in the stress. Maybe he got the random text to meet me, left the iron on in his haste, and burned down his shop. Benedikt's death was an accident. Security could only improve without Petras. We didn't know who stole the client list, but it was safe. Giacomo was involved, but he seemed just as on edge about it.

Things were looking up.

Nineteen

Lio

S WEATY, STARVING, AND EXHAUSTED, I finally entered the lobby of the main building. The misters washed over me, and I paused under the fans, letting their spray work its magic for a moment. The cool didn't last long. As I waved to Cooper and turned the corner to the elevators, a chill ran up my spine as heat flushed my cheeks.

"Hey, Lio," I said, stopping a dozen tiles away.

He stood from the leather bench, wearing a loose tank top and pink shorts so tight, I could tell he wasn't wearing underwear. "I was worried, Mister Matteo. I heard the fire alarm and couldn't get ahold of you."

"I've been very busy," I said, eyeing the elevator call button only a few feet away.

"Of course. You must be hungry. Let me make you something. Maybe rub you down before bed." He grinned, but all his flirting only brought forward my anger. I so badly wanted to end my day with him, but not without knowing why he'd lied to me. That wasn't a truth I was ready for.

"I should spend the night alone," I said

I stepped toward the call button, and he matched my movement.

"I don't have to stay. Just let me come up for a bit to make you feel better."

"No, Lio."

He flinched, but it quickly melted into a grin, and he stabbed the elevator button. "Give me twenty minutes to make that a yes."

"Go home, Lio."

The doors opened with a soft chime.

He genuinely shied back a step. "Did I do something wrong?"

I snorted. "Fucking hell. The number of guys I've heard that from. You know what you did, and you only ask because you don't want to give away something else I might not be aware of."

"Please, Mister Matteo." His pleading tone tried its best to melt the ice around my heart.

I stared into the elevator car, watching the doors slide shut. "Fine. How did you get back into my suite last night? It's supposed to require a key."

Emotions warred through Lio, staring at my shoes—surprise, shock, guilt. I'd seen it before. He was trying to decide what and how much I knew. He had to say something, but what would be the minimum?

He pushed the call button again and nodded for me to follow. "Holding the open and close buttons when you press the floor gets around the security."

He pushed the buttons as he spoke, and doors slid shut. "Your father taught me the override."

"You invited yourself up to visit my father? What did Herr Jensen think about that?"

Lio's eyes were wide, lunging a step toward me but backing off just as quickly. "It's not like that. Your father and I... we, we never... I mean, I helped him to relax now and then, but it was nothing more than running his bath or rubbing his feet. I just delivered things for him. It's my job, delivering things. Things he didn't want left at the front desk."

The elevator opened to my suite. "What kinds of things?" I shifted to lean against the doors to keep them from closing.

"All sorts. Small packages, heavy things. Everything was wrapped, so I don't know." He was rambling.

"Did you ever see my father with anyone as you let yourself into the suite?" I don't know why I asked it, other than some tiny lingering question after watching his farewell video.

Lio rubbed a hand across his stubbled jaw, then through his hair. He sucked in a deep breath. "I'm only telling you this because I don't want you to think I'm holding anything back. Mister Andretti would be up there at any hour, and when I'd see him in the morning, he looked like he'd stayed the night."

A relationship between my father and the lawyer didn't mean much other than to explain some of Andretti's desire for La Luce's success. It wasn't just his life's work, but his lover's, too. They built La Luce together and Andretti would see that complete.

I backed into my room, and Lio, shoulders low, followed to take my place, blocking the door sensor.

"I didn't kill him," Lio whispered at my shoes. "I loved Benedikt and would have once given him everything that is me, but he made it impossible. Enzo tried to get between us, thinking he'd suddenly defend the father he hated and..." He paused, rubbing his forehead. "Enzo and I agreed to say nothing. It truly was an accident."

"Yet you tried really hard last night to make me suspicious of him."

"I was scared, Mister Matteo." Lio shuffled forward, and the elevator whispered closed behind him. "It was happening so fast. I didn't know what to do."

I searched the pleading in Lio's wide eyes, perhaps hoping for some sign of deceit, but only saw a confused young man who got in over his head. "You should have both come forward immediately."

"I know." He reached for my shoulders but shied away again. "We panicked. We hoped it would look like an accident with no one else around."

"Murderers don't tend to stay hovering over their victims. They flee and hope not to get caught." I sighed. At least their stories aligned. Though, Enzo's was more violent. "I don't know if you're malicious, Lio. I hope you aren't. I want to like you. But you are opportunistic. Until I can get a clear head, we need to keep our distance. You're my employee, and... that's it." I pushed the call button, and the doors opened immediately with a chime.

Lio glanced over his shoulder to the waiting elevator car. "He wanted you out," he whispered, drawing me a hair nearer to hear him. "He respected your father but called Andretti a fool to search for you."

"You were defending me?"

"Benedikt was furious when he heard I saw you when you arrived, assuming what we'd done."

"He probably assumed right, but it's not his business if you two were broken up. You were fighting about me when Enzo tried to pull you apart?"

He nodded enthusiastically. "Yes. I tried to tell him how good you'll be for La Luce."

"Was Benedikt who you were warning me about? Those who don't want my success here?"

Lio shook his head. "Benedikt would have been vocal, complaining against you, but would never do anything." He shifted near enough for me to feel his heat and raised an arm to lean his elbow against the wall as the door closed again. It was all a display to show off his bicep, but I watched it. "You put your feet up while I run the bath and make you something to eat. That's all. Let me do my job." He tucked a thumb into his shorts, tugging them low enough to nearly flash his dick. I stared down at his exposed pubes.

Pete did this same shit for four months after we broke up. He'd show up to the apartment with some flimsy excuse. "I couldn't find something and thought I left it here." "Could you crack my back like only you can?" "I got this free bottle of wine." Being a dumbass, I'd always open the door. Then I'd let him in just enough to close it. He'd sprinkle just enough compliments with subtle hints at how he missed me. "Is this shirt new?" "Have you been going to the gym?" "I miss holding your hand." Before long, I got out the corkscrew and two wine glasses because, well, why not? He was here, and so was the wine. An hour later, we'd be in bed, and an hour after that, I'd be doing all I could to make him leave. Repeat all that within five to ten business days.

It took me four months to learn and end that behavior with Pete, and he wasn't a fraction as hot as Lio.

Snagging his hand from his waistband, I tugged him away from the elevator. "You're not staying the night."

"Of course not," he said, slipping my hand down his shorts onto his rapidly growing member.

Our shirts only made it a few steps as we fumbled and tripped across the plush carpet. Lips pressed against the other's or trailed across our jaws and necks. Our hands struggled with belts. This was the raw passion we'd lacked last night, that carnal lust where we couldn't get close enough to the other. Naked, bodies crushing together, fingertips caressing and gripping.

We blindly found our way to the bed, knocking over the dividing screen with a dull crash, and I shoved him back to the sheets, forcing my way in to stand between his knees. He lay propped up on his elbows, chest heavy and glistening with anticipation. Fucking hell, he was a sight with his hair a mess, lips parted, and abs tightening with every breath. How would we do this? I wanted to taste every inch of him, wanted to make him moan and shout things I didn't understand. He could bottom again, this time with me on top. Or I could try taking him. We could take turns. We could move to the couch, the balcony, the dining table.

That stupid, fucking, nagging voice came forward, saying that this wasn't me. That there was a power balance here. That I should be getting settled, not fucking the hot guy that wanted to be my valet. Yeah, fuck it, he got the job. So what about his lies and omissions? I'd fucked plenty of guys on the first date, even more on the second, so why was I pausing here?

Because this wasn't a date, and Lio was an employee.

I stepped back, rubbing my hands over my face as the fog of lust faded.

"Mister Matteo?" Lio pushed to his palms.

"Things are moving too fast, Lio. I'm sorry. You can stay the night, but we need to slow down."

He sat up and reached for my hand. "Don't apologize, Mister Matteo. I'll run you a bath." He kissed my fingers and stood, letting his palm slide around my hip as he passed.

First, there was regret for stopping a night of incredible sex, then pride for the same, for returning to myself. I wouldn't let a wave of teenage hormones make the decisions. My dick was not the boss of me.

The microwave beeped, pulling me back. Lio slid a small plate onto the kitchen island and returned toward the bathroom, still naked, sucking on his fingers one at a time. I walked over and stared down at the high-end Hot Pocket. He knew I was hungry, that this would be the ideal little snack. Lio closed a cabinet in the bathroom with a quiet bang, and I noticed the wetness on my face. Was I crying? What the fuck was wrong with me? Lio was either extremely considerate or just really good at his job, but it was enough to move me to tears. It might have all been his act to manipulate me, but I pushed down that little nagging idea. The heat and stress were wrecking my emotions.

That wasn't it. It was Pete again and all the shit-head boyfriends that came and went through my life. I'd always been the nice one who didn't argue. He'd always get his way. Picking the movie and where we went for dinner. It was always what he wanted to do. When I finally stood up for myself, demanding he pay for dinner occasionally, clean the apartment, or let me pick the radio station, he'd snap, call me a selfish queen, and things would tumble away from there.

This steaming ham and cheese wrap showed that Lio wanted to care for me, no matter his reason. What would it feel like not to have to drag the other toward the center? To be with someone who wanted to please as much as I always had? That wasn't quite right. It wasn't that I wanted to please my partner, but I wanted someone who would pull their weight. Pete and the others wanted a parent, not a partner. Someone to manage the bills, do the laundry, and make the appointments while they went out with friends I didn't know and spent every cent they made. Lio's motives weren't as clear, or maybe I didn't want to see or accept them.

Wiping a palm across my eyes, I followed the sound of running water and the smell of rose oil and sandalwood. With the lights dimmed, Lio perched on the tub's edge, just as he had yesterday, running his fingers through the water. We spoke in the language of gestures and glances. I stepped into the water, and Lio slid in behind me. His strong fingers moved slowly, finding the stress in my shoulders and neck, and his lips trailed in their wake. Mine stroked and massaged his calves and thighs wrapped around my waist.

That nagging voice returned, warning this was worse than fucking. That this intimacy heralded something that could never happen, or at least shouldn't.

I shut it out, reaching back for a careful fistful of Lio's hair, pulling him closer until his breath tickled my neck. His ministrations ended, and he wrapped me in his arms with a few delicate kisses behind my ear.

"When did you know you wanted more from Benedikt?" I asked. "Was it a single moment, or did you feel it grow?"

Lio tensed behind me but melted with the next breath. "It was a moment."

"Tell me about it."

He tensed again, and his fingers fidgeted on my stomach. "It would be a graphic story."

"Tell me," I said, rubbing his thigh. "Please."

"Well, I... I told you that Benedikt liked watching me with other men, right?"

I nodded.

"He invited a couple not unlike us, an older man and his boy. Benedikt sat beside the man while I and the other..."

I felt this chest heave beneath me. "You don't have to tell me if it's too difficult," I said, unable to dismiss the charm in his awkward modesty, especially while we were naked in a tub.

"I think I want to," he said, breathing slowly against my back. "We kissed and pulled off each other's clothes. I was blowing him when he signaled he wanted me to fuck him. So I did. I never knew anyone could howl and moan that loud, but he swore I wasn't hurting him. We had a safe word, just in case. After a few minutes of shifting between positions, the other older man came over, taking out his dick as he did. The boy grabbed for it, furiously sucking him. I was soon forgotten, and I don't think he noticed when I pulled out. Benedikt watched the two of them finish each other, never looking my way."

Goddamn. When Lio told me that Benedikt liked to watch, I didn't devote the mental energy to envision that. Now that he painted the picture in stark oils on canvas, I saw how fucked their relationship was.

"I wanted what they had," Lio said. "Well, not exactly that, needing a third to finish each other, but they were so tender together in the end. Benedikt said he loved me, but I never felt what those two must have."

He heard the words but never felt it. I'd been there, too. Fuck, I'd said it without meaning it, but I promised myself years ago never to do that again.

When would I next say it?

"Thank you for telling me," I whispered, sliding down another inch and pushing into his core.

Lio heaved a breath and squeezed, chuckling nervously. "I haven't told anyone else that. It felt good, like a weight off my chest or a breath I'd been holding all these months." He kissed my neck. "Are you ready for the meeting tomorrow?"

"No, but I'm not doing anything more about that tonight."

"How about some TV? There's a new season of Paul Hollywood."

I spun to face Lio, splashing water over the tub's lip. "You watch Bake Off?"

"Every season," he winked.

I fell into those gray eyes, leaning to kiss him. It was always the little things that made a relationship special, and he was starting strong: making a Hot Pocket, a shared love of British reality baking shows, moments of vulnerability.

He couldn't stay on as my valet, but there had to be a hundred other jobs for him within La Luce. He could be an engineer at the water and power plant or a chef.

It was fucking Pete again. I'd get him a different job so we could be together. I'd get him cleared of any manslaughter charges after he lied to me about where he was.

But as much as this was the same as every terrible, toxic man before, he was just as different. Sure, he was rife with flaws, but who wasn't? And the little moments of mindfulness compounded to chip through and show me the glimmer of his radiant core.

When did I last have to be so fucking literary to justify going to bed with someone?

"Let me get your back first," I said.

Lio spread his easy grin and spun away.

Twenty

Testament

A TEXT ALERT STARTLED me awake. The night was a blur, and though I didn't remember having any dreams, the sweaty sheets spoke otherwise. I checked the time first—almost eight—and saw the message from Andretti. At least he might be getting the hint that my generation preferred text over cold calls.

> Marco Andretti: Petras did not go quietly, but he is gone, and the ports have been reopened. I also have positive news regarding last night's incident. Come to my office. Call me when you are on your way.

"Last night's incident" meaning a fire that decimated one of the key shops in the resort. Maybe the news is that it was confirmed not to be arson, which was good, considering my current situation.

Dropping my phone beside the pillow, I rolled to face Lio. Laying with one arm tossed over his head and the other across his ribs, the sheets tangled around his knees. I traced a finger down his side, following the outline of his blue fish tattoo ridged with muscle. Continuing to his hip and across his groin, the flat of my palm spread fingers across his bare thigh.

We'd stayed up too late on the couch, cheering on the contestants and judging their baked creations despite neither of us having a fraction of their skill. Lio had been the one responsible for finally ushering us to bed.

With my palm still on his thigh, I curled my fingers to brush up the underside of his balls. They reacted, the skin tightening. Lio took a deep breath and shifted his arm but didn't wake.

Seriously, what was wrong with me? Since first stepping foot on this island, my head hadn't been on straight. My life was threatened, a man was dead, another's work burned to coals, and rather than reacting to the message that might lead to answers, I was fondling a sleeping man in my bed—a man implicated in a death and who admitted to lying to my direct questions.

Yet, my fingertip skimmed slowly, achingly so, down Lio's member to the tip of his foreskin. I could wake my sexy porter to do what we hadn't done last night and tell Andretti I hadn't seen his text right away. I was suffering from jet lag. I could just...

I mentally slapped myself and rolled away, snatching my phone and landing on my feet. Seconds later, I was hunched over the bathroom sink, splashing cold water over my face. Staring down at the pool in my cupped hands, I knew something was very wrong. This was more than the heat, long days, and scenery of beautiful men. I wasn't right in the head here. But, few things were solved by staring into water.

I would solve something, though.

My time in La Luce started with me wanting to trust Lio, but I realized now, a day later, that was childish. I wanted to trust him because he was hot and seemed interested in me. It was like I was in middle school and wanted to make friends with the jock. No, I had to be friends with the teacher, with the principal. The superintendent.

Pulling on a pair of linen pants, I put the client list in one front pocket and the USB drive with surveillance videos in the other. I wouldn't leave my meeting with Andretti without giving him at least one, if not both. That would be the plan, at least.

Buttoning up my loose shirt, I peeked around the screen at Lio. He was every erotic photographer's wet dream; how casual he looked while stirring a primal, feral lust within me. Early morning light shone through the windows at a low angle, casting shadows across the valleys of Lio's core, and it took every shred of willpower not to lean down to kiss him farewell. He might be toxic, and he might exemplify all my poor decisions in men, but he also might be the best thing to happen to me in years. It was too early to know. Either way, he was a whole lot more to look at and listen to. I could slip in beside him, delay Andretti another few minutes...

I took the ankh necklace from the nightstand, fidgeting with the clasp, weighing if I should continue wearing it. No, I'd made that decision last night when I told Lio he could stay. I slipped the necklace on and bent to kiss him on the cheek.

He stirred as I rounded the screen separating the bed from the rest of the suite.

"Going somewhere, Mister Matteo?" He'd rolled to his side with an arm draped over his stomach.

I wanted that arm over my stomach... "Andretti needs me. Sleep as late as you want."

He flipped to his belly, sliding across the sheets toward me with his sculpted ass popped in the air. "Do you have to go right now? Let me get you a coffee."

What harm would a twenty-minute delay make? Andretti didn't sound at all rushed in his text. Twenty minutes here would lead to thirty minutes in the shower and another twenty in the bathroom and... This wasn't me. I'd never had a Lio throwing himself at me like this, but I always thought I had enough work ethic to prioritize myself better.

"Let me get this done first, Lio. We can reconnect this afternoon." I lifted his chin to press my lips to his, turning away before the pleading in his eyes had me unbuttoning my shirt.

I texted Andretti from the elevator, telling him I was on my way. His office was a three-minute walk, and he replied, "Thank you," as I pushed into the office suite.

The row of private, fully-equipped offices were likely meant for men who came to La Luce but weren't able to leave their work at home. Each had a white oak desk on par with the one in the Oval Office. Ridiculous and indulgent, but for who La Luce might attract, it might be completely expected to have nothing less. The last door in the white wainscotted hall showed a gold plaque with "Macro Andretti, Esq" stamped into it. I knocked twice.

"Enter."

I could barely hear him through the mahogany door.

A wall of windows across the back of Andretti's office looked out over a pond with a fountain spraying a rainbow in the morning light. The desk and accompanying full-grain leather chair were empty. My eyes ran over the silver and glass table holding a half dozen decanters of whiskeys or rums, the bookshelves stuffed with tomes reaching the ceiling twelve feet up, and an oil painting that might have been Carmelo's home fishing village. I almost jumped when I finally took enough of it in to notice the leather couch to my right and Andretti sitting with an ankle crossed over his knee. He wore another classic look of wool and silk, no doubt made by the late Herr Jensen, and rolled an unlit cigar in his fingers.

But he was not alone. The other was sitting in the chair opposite Andretti, leaning forward with his elbows on his knees, running his hands through his wild mop of hair.

"Enzo, good morning," I said. What does one say to a person whose father died and his business went up in smoke?

Andretti waved me to the third seat facing them. "Mister Jensen was telling me—"

"I fucked it, Matteo. I left that iron on. I got so worked up, have been so worked up. It was an accident." He bit his thumbnail, focusing on his shoes.

Between Enzo not looking up and the nervous bob of his knee, I heard his confession as carefully scripted, if poorly executed. I started imagining Andretti threatening Enzo before I walked in, demanding he play along or the lawyer would bring down some additional ruin on the tailor. Had I always been this paranoid?

"The optics and timing could hardly be worse," said Andretti. "The investors, especially Signor Barbieri, will demand assurance that this will not happen again."

"How do you assure a fire will never happen?" I asked.

Andretti set the cigar on the coffee table between us all. "Signor Barbieri is not known for always being responsible."

"You have a shop in Xemxmarina, too, right? Santiago told me you split time between them with your father."

Enzo nodded but didn't look up. "The original."

"You know I think you're innocent, Enzo," I said. "But I have to ask: Why were you in the resort? Santiago said it was your father's shift."

"They're both my shops. I go where I fucking want."

"I'm not a cop, Enzo. I'm trying to paint a picture."

He huffed loudly. "Fine, complete honesty? I was hoping to run into you. I wanted to get to you before him. If I could be the one to clothe the next owner, I'd win."

"Why did you kick me out, then? You told me to fuck off so you could get back to work."

"My old man would be back any second. It was just luck that you walked in when you did, when I was in the back arranging crap, but I needed to cover my tracks that I was there. Not that I was doing anything wrong, being in my own shop."

"Quite endearing, Mister Jensen," said Andretti. "The facility within La Luce held about one-third of the total material stock but most of the completed wares. This is recoverable, but the timetable for re-building the shop before the grand opening is near impossible."

"Near impossible means it could be done," I said.

"It can't," said Enzo, bouncing his knee. "Even if all the building materials were magically tele-ported to the site along with an around-the-clock crew, there's nothing to put in it. I could pull stock from Xemxmarina, but that's mostly fabric samples. Everything my old man made was custom. I made the stuff in the resort, saying we needed to offer off-the-rack options. Last I checked, I'm not Snow White with magic birds to make clothes."

"That was Cinderella with mice," I said.

"I never actually saw either," said Enzo.

Someone knocked twice.

"Enter," Andretti nearly screamed to be heard.

A thin young man in a pink polo and blue shorts pushed open the door without a word and offered Andretti a thick manila envelope. The lawyer accepted it, and I noticed Enzo lifting his gaze to follow.

"Thank you, Jace," said Andretti, dismissing the page without looking at him as he did. As soon as the door clicked closed, Andretti reached over to twist the deadlock, then ripped open the top of the envelope. "I have been waiting for this." He pulled out a stack of comb-bound white paper, opening it to somewhere near the second half.

"It's not in there," said Enzo, shifting farther forward. "Please, Baby Jesus, don't be in there."

"What?" I asked.

Andretti flipped through the papers, wetting his fingertip to unstick them as needed. He quickly turned the stack so I could read the front.

The Last Will and Testament of Benedikt Martin Jensen.

"It just came to my attention that Herr Jensen updated his will three months ago," Andretti said. "This was a surprise because I had been handling his paperwork for years. He—"

Andretti spat a string of syllables I was sure my translation app would show as all asterisks. He handed the will to Enzo, pointing to a line, and the tailor repeated the swears but in a heavy Chicago accent.

"Benedikt Jensen amassed his fortune from nothing, using only his skill with a needle and tape measure," said Andretti, speaking slowly. "He made Isola di Luce a destination for the world's elite who would pay a king's ransom to be clothed in a Jensen Classic. When Rafael Demetriou came to the island, Herr Jensen embraced him and became one of the resort's first investors."

Enzo threw the will onto the coffee table and let his head sink between his knees.

Andretti continued. "Despite their myriad issues, Enzo Jensen had always been his father's beneficiary. But he updated his will three months ago." He slid the papers toward me, tapping at a line.

Twenty-One

Kin

I COULD READ THE text in front of Andretti's finger, but I still pushed forward in my chair to get a few inches closer to verify I wasn't mistaken. "Lio Dante Carbone? My Lio? The porter?"

Enzo glanced up at Andretti, but his eyes narrowed on me. "*Your* Lio? That slut gets around. It wasn't enough that he stole my father's fortune, my fortune, but now he's going after yours. He'll own all of La Luce before he's thirty." He snatched up the papers. "At least I get the shops, if not any of the capital or investitures or the villa."

"Perhaps he did that knowing you could rebuild on your own," I said.

"And maybe I could if half the business wasn't currently smoldering coal."

"Product was ruined, and the storefront sustained water and smoke damage," said Andretti. "No one was harmed, and no intellectual property was impugned. The repair crews will be on site tomorrow evening."

Enzo tossed the will onto the table. "Is that supposed to make me feel better?"

"I am merely pointing out your overreaction. The business accounts are in your name now, enough to rebuild and carry on for a year, at least." Andretti collected the will, folding it back to its cover page. "Mister Jensen, we will contest this. That your father went to an outside firm could imply coercion."

Enzo glowered at the lawyer. "We both know that's not true. Lio's a dumbfuck who couldn't coerce his way out of a paper bag. He just slaps his dick around to get what he wants."

"What we know does not matter in court, Mister Jensen. Your father made a major alteration to his will without informing his beneficiary or lawyer."

Enzo huffed. "This better not get anywhere near a courtroom."

"Do we believe the porter is aware of this?" Andretti asked, looking between me and Enzo.

"No," I said. "Lio wanted to end things with Benedikt."

"As if you can believe anything he says," Enzo scoffed. "He knew, and that's why he shoved my old man onto the rocks."

"He didn't shove him or trip him," I said a little too quickly. "It was an accident."

"I wanted to like you, Matteo, but you're a fucking moron if you're gobbling up everything that idiot says."

I wanted to give Enzo a second blackeye but knew he was speaking from rage. Fine... I'd planned on only showing Andretti, but it also pertained to Enzo.

He and I would have to function together, which wouldn't work with him at my throat. He wasn't going anywhere, and I had no plans to leave. I dug the USB drive from my pocket, holding it up between them. "Unless he can carefully edit video, I believe him."

"Would you care to elaborate, Mister Demetriou?" Andretti asked with his eyebrows high.

"I've only been here two nights, and I can see it'll take some time to get used to the shadowy politics within La Luce."

"Speak plainly," said Andretti.

"Yeah, what the hell is that supposed to mean?" asked Enzo.

"Before you see what's on this, no, I have no idea who gave it to me. It was wrapped and left poolside under my balcony. They sent an anonymous message telling me to look for it." I wrapped my fingers around the little bit of plastic, squeezing it in a fist. "There was footage of the zen garden two nights ago. This is how I can speak with any assurance about what happened. Enzo, you may not want to watch."

The tailor huffed a deep breath, setting his jaw. I thought I was pretty clear in implying, "This is a video of your father dying," but Enzo nodded, ready to bear the weight of whatever he might watch.

"I think I should see this," said Andretti.

I dropped the flash drive into his hand and followed them to the desk. The lawyer pushed the drive into the side of the monitor and dropped into the chair. His screen was the same confusing operating system, but within seconds, we were staring at the list of folders, each for a different camera.

Andretti slipped on a pair of reading glasses from beside the monitor. "What am I looking at, Mister Demetriou?"

"There are two files at the root. Open the larger one."

Using a trackpad on the edge of the keyboard, Andretti scrolled to the bottom of the list and hovered over the file but paused. Slipping off the glasses, he turned to face us. "With no chain of custody, nothing contained on this drive is admissible in court. Whatever we are about to witness is for our eyes only, for personal use. For educational purposes."

Enzo snapped his fingers, sharp and piercing. "Enough lawyering. Open it."

Andretti swung back to the screen, donned his glasses, and clicked the video file.

I'd watched it a dozen times or more, knew all the cue points, and exactly when to take a long blink to miss Benedikt hitting the ground. Rather, his head cracking against the rock. The first time had been enough. I didn't watch the video this time, but studied how Andretti and Enzo reacted. The former hardly blinked, never showing a break in his quiet temper. He understood what he was watching, and after I left the frame, he increased the playback speed until Lio and Benedikt entered.

Enzo's anger melted away, uncrossing his arms as he recognized the scene. His fist clenched as Lio fought with his father, he touched his swollen eye when Lio hit him, and gasped, clapping a hand over his eyes when his father fell. Enzo turned to the wall of windows, hands gripping his hair.

Andretti leaned closer, drawing the video back, stepping through the frames. After a few minutes of analysis, he closed the video and set his glasses on the desk to pinch his nose. He didn't look at me as he asked, "When did you receive this?"

"Yesterday evening."

"Before or after the fire?"

"Before."

Enzo whirled on me, grabbing my elbow to face him. "You had this before we talked on the beach? That's why you defended Lio so strongly. You were trying to play detective, weren't you? Trying to catch me—"

"That's enough, Mister Jensen," Andretti said quietly but with the gravitas to end Enzo's tirade. Mister Demetriou has offered this to us, so do not stress the timeliness—or lack thereof." He finally looked up at me. "Is the second video relevant?"

Was it? Andretti and Enzo both knew Lio was the third man in the video. Showing him leaving and returning to my suite had given me clarity in what I was seeing, but would add nothing for them beyond opening the door for questions about why the shirtless porter was fleeing to my room. I couldn't withhold from them now, though.

"It shows Lio left my suite shortly before the fight and returned after. The video's cut to make it clear that's what it's highlighting."

"He fled back to your suite covered in my father's blood?" Enzo asked, holding back an awkward laugh.

"Did you fuck him? I bet it was good, him still on the high from killing my old man, knowing he'd just inherited his fortune."

"Enough!" Andretti slammed a fist on his desk, shooting to his feet. "Mister Jensen, I suggest you take a quiet vacation away from the island for a few weeks. Let your emotions settle while I develop a plan to contest the will. Meanwhile, no one is to discuss it outside the three of us. The easiest route would be to throw out this updated version, which will be easier if no one is aware to fight that."

Don't tell Lio he's technically a multi-millionaire, got it.

"I would like to keep this drive, Mister Demetriou. I may be able to extract metadata to give us a clue as to who sent this. Even if it is nothing more than a workstation where the second video was edited."

"It was probably Petras," said Enzo, walking around to the other side of the desk. "He was on someone's payroll and tried to cover this up. It's the same as having no cameras on my shop. But one of his goons knew this was too big and slipped you the footage."

Andretti leaned forward with his palms on the desk. "Reasonable, but unprovable as of yet. Is this the only copy, Mister Demetriou?"

I nodded. I couldn't figure out the operating system to make copies. "Is there a Noah in security?"

Enzo rolled his eyes and faced back to the window, but Andretti raised a finger to scratch his temple. "I believe there is a Noah Gomez. Why?"

How could I explain why I knew his name without suddenly divulging what I'd overheard from the bathroom at the party? Why should I keep that to myself? I'd been upset with Andretti for spoon-feeding me information, yet here I was. "No reason."

Andretti stared at his monitor for a moment, then pushed back from the desk. "Mister Jensen, please give us the room."

Enzo spread his arms, questioning, but said nothing. He waved an arm at us and stormed from the office.

"The client list," Andretti said when the door had barely closed. "Mister Jensen was correct in saying Petras was on someone's take. Whoever printed the client list did so with Petras' help. It's crystal clear to me."

My fingers brushed my pocket, feeling the stiffness of the paper beneath the thin linen. "Any progress on that?"

He shook his head. "The ports are open, so the list may well have left on the first boat. We can only hope the culprit contacts us for a ransom before taking action."

"Would we pay a ransom? Doesn't that just encourage more?"

"We have insurance."

I slipped my thumb into my pockets, touching the folded printout. I could hand the page to Andretti right then and end the mystery—or at least the danger. He would ask how it came into my possession, which could lead to exposing Agent Alec. Would it really be so bad for the lawyer to know that Interpol was creeping around the island?

Andretti spoke before I mustered my courage, deciding for me. "You should see yourself out, Mister Demetriou. The meeting with the investors is in..." He shook out his watch to check the time. "Christ, less than three hours away. I need to make headway on Herr Jensen's will, as I have no doubt that will come up."

My thumb left my pockets, and the client list remained safely within. "I've read all their info. I'll be ready."

He stopped me halfway to the door.

"Thank you." His words were a whisper, and I turned back to him, his palms still flat on the desk. "Though these videos cause more questions than they answer, it is a relief to know there was nothing overtly malicious about Herr Jensen's death. We were colleagues and business partners for so long, I have yet to understand how to process his passing. This helps."

I nodded and turned, but he spoke again when my hand touched the doorknob.

"And, Mister Demetriou, do not let the extravagance of La Luce overwhelm you. Do not lose yourself to poor decisions."

I was sure that was lawyer-speak for, "Stop fucking the porter," but I only nodded again and saw myself out.

Andretti had a thousand things to do before the investor meeting, but the only thing I could think of was reading through the paperwork once more.

Maybe I'd go for a swim in one of the dozen pools or see what food offerings there were. Surely, the owner wouldn't have to subsist on microwaved chicken nuggets and instant ramen.

I stepped into the day's growing heat, squinting at the sun. The breeze would keep down the humidity, but this would take some getting used to.

"Hey," Enzo said behind me.

I spun to him, leaning on the wall beside the doors. He pushed off and got close enough that I could see the gold flecks in his eyes. If he intended to hit me, he'd succeed.

"That got pretty intense in there," he said. "I'm sure you can understand. It's been a lot."

His father dies, he burned down his shop, then learned his father left everything to his... his what? Lover? Partner? You don't leave everything to someone you didn't hope to live the rest of your life with.

"For what it's worth, I'm sorry, Matteo. I said some nasty shit in there that I shouldn't have."

I'd been the butt of enough outbursts to know accepting the apology meant you agreed they were wrong, which led to another layer of the fight. Brushing it off was a better choice.

"There's nothing to be sorry about, Enzo. You've—"

With a viper's speed, he snatched the silver chain around my neck, pulling the ankh pendant into the morning sunlight. "But what in the ever-loving fuck is this about, Matteo? You know Lio gave my old man one of these, and now he's branded you, too? Don't think I didn't notice this when you came into my shop the other day, only minutes after you landed on the island." He dropped the ankh and crossed his arms but didn't step back.

I could repeat the story Lio told me in the tub last night, but was pretty sure Enzo didn't want to hear it.

"Look, it's your business who you put your dick in, or vice versa, but if you're going to be our fearless leader, think about how it looks for you to... that." He waved his hand, dismissing his thought. "I don't like Lio and never will, especially now. Let's just hope Andretti can do something about the will, but a vacation right before the big, stressful grand opening sounds nice. Maybe a train ride through the Alps. I'll send you a postcard. *Addio*." He snapped his fingers, shooting me double guns, and turned on a heel. His shoulders drooped a little more with each step.

"Wait," I called, jogging to catch up. Enzo plastered on his grin as he turned. "Was it really an accident?" I asked.

His grin soured. "You'll have to be more specific. Are you asking about the death of my father or the destruction of my livelihood? I suppose that will be one and the same once Lio takes over and Jensen Classics begins producing cargo shorts, logo snapbacks, and polyester everything."

I asked for that. "The fire. You sounded, I don't know, *off* in there."

"And you know me so well to know when I'm *on*?"

"Enzo, please, I'm sorry. I'm only trying to understand what's going on around here."

He rolled his eyes and heaved a long breath. "You're wondering if I did it on purpose to collect the insurance and free myself from the island? Or is someone threatening me? Scaring me to force my hand like an R-rated episode of Scooby Doo? If it's the first, I'm not tipping my hand by telling you, and if it's the second, be glad I don't involve you as I keep my mouth shut."

I waited for him to say more, but a dozen heartbeats passed in silence.

"You won't confirm it wasn't either of those?" I asked.

"I don't like repeating myself for someone hoping to get a different answer out of me, Matteo. I would testify to what I said in Andretti's office. Leave it at that."

I never imagined someone being so aggressive when telling the truth, but Enzo needed time to cool down before I could start fresh with him. "Good luck, Enzo."

"Sure. You too." He flicked me a wave and turned again to leave.

Twenty-Two

List

ANDRETTI MIGHT BE LOSING his mind, but the best thing I could do would be staying out of his way. Though... Maybe it wasn't...

I slid the paper from my pocket. Other than when Alec first handed it to me on the beach, I'd only unfolded it enough to confirm the blood spots, that it was indeed the same piece of paper. Holding it out in the morning sun, I scanned over the names crammed onto the page. There was no header across the top to identify what the list was. There was no contact information or arrival dates—just six groups of ten names and a few at the bottom that looked garbled by digital corruption.

This was tabloid fodder. It might make the front page of a trashy magazine at the supermarket checkout, but no reputable news organization would touch this. The longer I stared at it, searching for a name I recognized, the more laughable it became.

Alec weaved a wild tale of a shootout on the north shore on par with the O.K. Corral, but Andretti said no one was hit. The agent's hand had been wrapped...

I imagined him hovering over the sheet of paper, wincing as he pierced his palm, staging the list with his own blood.

Were any shots fired? What if Petras and Alec were working together to spread that rumor?

This wasn't a piece of paper to bring down a hundred-million-dollar resort; it was a red herring. It was the symbol of a security breach but worthless to anyone outside the island. That meant whoever tried to use it was responsible for it.

Giacomo Barbieri knew about it and wanted it enough to beat the shit out of Noah.

Goddammit, Noah. I hoped he was okay.

I yanked open the door to the office suite and stormed down the wainscotted hall, soft shoes slapping on the polished marble. I knew what I had to do and would see it through before I talked myself out of it. Knocking twice on the door, I didn't wait for a response before pushing it open.

"Mister Demetriou," Andretti looked flustered between me and the phone in his hand. He spat Italian into it and slammed the receiver down. "What is the meaning of this? That was a very import—" He cut off when I dropped the client list on the desk before him. Picking it up, he cringed at the blood and slowly raised his gaze to me, brow knit tight. "Is this what I think it is?"

"The client list. I was told that is the only copy."

"How?"

"Quid pro quo, Andretti. I want an answer from you first. You said my father died from ALS, Santiago said it was suicide, and you amended your story to agree with him. Others say it was murder. Which was it, and am I in danger?"

Andretti leaned back with a heavy sigh, rubbing a hand over his head. "Have a seat." He waved to the couches by the door and pushed up to pour drinks from the decanters I'd noticed earlier. "In short, no. Your father was not murdered."

"How can you be so sure? You said he was seen going into the lighthouse and never came out. What if someone was waiting for him in there?"

Andretti handed me the rocks glass with a few fingers of whiskey and sat across from me. "Because I was the last one to see him alive." He held his drink between his knees, watching it swirl. "This is not easy for me, Mister Demetriou. My generation did not allow men to have or show emotion. We were told we could only cry three times in our lives: at the birth of our first son, at our mother's funeral, and when our team won the World Cup." He gulped back his drink in one go. "I feel no shame in saying I cried that night after I left your father alone in the lighthouse. I helped him to climb the stairs, knowing what he meant to do once he got to the top, but nothing I said convinced him out of it." Andretti leaned forward, elbows on his knees, clasping his head.

"Fuck." I shot my drink and got up for the bottle. "His disease was that bad that he wanted to end it? What did the doctors say?"

Andretti snorted. "Rafael detested doctors. Doctor Ricci diagnosed him but questioned the speed of progression. I spoke with the best medical researchers across Europe. They all agreed, but your father refused to submit to their tests."

"Is that why there are the rumors of murder?"

Andretti looked up as I poured him another glass. "What does that mean? You cannot use ALS to murder someone. There are possible genetic markers that can make one more susceptible, and environmental factors may trigger it, but it is not communicable."

"That's more than I meant, sorry. What if someone triggered it? Or if it was something else with all the symptoms, but Ricci got it wrong without more testing?"

Andretti pulled a cell phone from his pants pocket, swiping and tapping quickly while I watched his eyes scan left to right as he read.

"Thallium poisoning can present similar to ALS—muscle atrophy, loss of coordination, speech issues—and progresses much more quickly." He tossed the phone onto the table in front of him before slumping back and finishing his drink in one go.

"Maybe that's it then. He could have been poisoned."

"Do you honestly think this never crossed my mind, Mister Demetriou? Do you imagine your father ingesting rat poison with dinner?"

I shrugged. "I don't imagine much at all about him. He ran off when I was ten."

"We will speak on that when we have time." He drummed fingers on his knee. "No, I researched every possible diagnosis, but was forced to take the doctors at their word."

"Doctors that never got to see him. This seems right up Giacomo's alley."

"I would have said Vera. But, we will never know. A twenty-second internet search cannot replace the medical tests that were never done. To answer your question, to the best of my knowledge, your father jumped from the lighthouse that night. The currents on the island's north end are treacherous. Nothing that goes in at night stays until dawn. You are not in similar danger."

"Unless he was poisoned with thallium, and they come after me next."

"Enough of this, Matteo." Andretti closed his eyes with a deep breath. "If you read your paperwork more closely, you would know that upon your death, all investitures fall to me, and trust that I wouldn't have brought you here just to kill you. The party would give you demands before they begin a poisoning regimen. Now tell me, how did you come upon the client list?"

Here we go. "Just after I arrived, before we met for dinner, an Interpol agent gave it to me on the beach." I sucked in a breath and held up a palm to stop his outburst of questions, but Andretti only raised an eyebrow. "I can't verify he is who he said, and as much as I'm starting to doubt it, seeing holes in his story, I don't want to give up his identity."

"I have been giving myself an ulcer over something you have had in your pocket for a day and a half." He rolled his glass across his forehead. "Like the surveillance video, you should have come to me immediately, but I suppose late is better than never at all."

"I don't see why this is so important or powerful. It's just a list of names. I could think up sixty men I'd like to smear without pausing. The list itself is meaningless, but it represents a flaw in La Luce. I figure whoever stole it, whoever orchestrated it, will try to use it."

Andretti set his second drink on the coffee table, untouched. "That was my first thought when Petras informed me, but I have been playing along." He leaned back and lightly tapped his cheek, staring at the wall above my head. "Giacomo Barbieri is the first and most obvious suspect, but it would have to be more than mere money for him. He has plenty of that."

"The wealthiest people in the world only want more money." I had dark thoughts about how I might wield La Luce for political power but kept those to myself. Giacomo might have similar plans.

Andretti groaned and pushed to his feet. "I'd like to end this conversation here. We can hypothesize and plot, but it is all a mental exercise, unlike our meeting in a few hours, which is very much real."

I wanted to hypothesize and plot with the old man, but I had nothing else to do, unlike him. "I'll see you soon, then. Let's try to be better allies in the future."

Back behind his desk, Andretti narrowed his eyes, then nodded. "Agreed."

Twenty-Three

Meeting

Lio WAS GONE WHEN I returned, but the bed was made and a silver carafe sat on the kitchen island with a cup and note beside it.

"Some more clothes came for you. I put them away in the closet. Breakfast is in the fridge. Good luck today!"

It was just missing an "xoxo" or heart.

I rubbed the note in my hand, feeling the indentations from the ballpoint pen with my thumb. Without thinking, I brought it to my nose, imagining I could smell Lio's woody cologne on it.

I really hoped Carmelo and the rest were wrong about Lio, that he was actually as tender and caring as he acted, as I wished him to be.

Pouring a cup of espresso, I checked the fridge, taking out the yogurt parfait with granola topped with fresh fruit and a cranberry tonic water to wash it down. While carrying it all and pushing the balcony door open with my hip, I couldn't think of a guy from my past who had done anything remotely like this, cleaning up and having breakfast ready. Maybe Lio was just doing his job, but he was doing it well. Maybe I did need a valet. I'd left to see Andretti without eating. I hadn't showered yet today, either. Things would only get more stressful after La Luce opened, though hopefully a different sort of stress, and maybe I would need someone to help me take care of myself.

With a full and happy belly, I stripped on my way to the bathroom, this time putting my clothes in the hamper rather than strewn on the floor. I took my time in the shower and after, making sure my hair was just right. My fingers walked through the new clothes hung up in the closet, picking out a light pale blue shirt to wear under a white one with green palm leaves stamped into it. When I found a nice pair of cream linen pants, I reconsidered the undershirt, then couldn't settle on shoes.

There was still more than an hour before the meeting, but I could do my language-learning game or sudoku there while I waited. The fifteen-minute walk would take me halfway across the resort to a conference center overlooking the eastern bluffs. Halfway there, sweat was dripping down my back, ruining all my careful work cultivating my look. I thought of the doctor's golf cart and how I might get one. I'm the owner; I should have one, right?

When I opened the glass door, I welcomed the blast of biting cold. An unmanned reception desk sat to my left, and a glass hallway stretched until it ended with a massive framed oil painting of my father. Why he was in the conference center would be a later question for the decorators.

I found the restroom, doing my best to recover from the heat. Splashing cold water on my face and arms helped, but my shirt would just have to dry.

My father's portrait grew in my vision as I approached it. He looked down his nose from eight feet up the wall. I didn't recognize the wall of books behind him as any place I'd visited yet in La Luce, but I'd hardly seen a fraction of the island, as tiny as it may be. Did he pose for the painting just outside the door before or after blackmailing a country into selling him the island and kicking off the last native? I turned away before he pulled me in, pushing open the last door on the right.

The wall of tinted windows provided a sweeping view of the Mediterranean Sea. Every window seemed to look out to water here. Gorgeous, yes, but I couldn't focus on any of that. I tested each of the dozen leather swivel chairs. Looking out the window without focus, I wondered where Petras was at that moment. Was he scrambling, knowing his blackmail and leverage on the island were now worthless? At least, I hoped that was the case if I'd understood my father's video correctly. So many questions, and I didn't even understand what I should be asking to get answers.

A change in air pressure pulled my attention back to the door, and Carmelo backed in with a serving cart.

"You're here early," he said and got to work setting out refreshments: a bottle of tonic water in front of nine chairs, a candy dish beside one, and mini pretzel rods by another.

"I thought I might show strength when everyone arrives and sees me already waiting for them," I said, tossing my feet on the table, ankles crossed, and nearly tipped backward.

"Careful, they could as easily think you have nothing better to do," he winked to soften his words, but he could be right. Though, so what? It's not wrong to say I was currently light on official tasks for the resort. The key word being "official." Maybe I'd be more than a mascot someday.

I watched Carmelo busy himself with lining the credenza at the head of the room with other finger snacks pulled from his cart. "Will you be here during the meeting?" I asked.

He didn't face me as he replied, "Usually yes. I've been the one to top off everyone's drinks in these meetings, but Mister Andretti was specific about there being no extra ears in the building."

Me, Andretti, Eli, Santiago, the four investors... "Who's the ninth chair for?"

Carmelo still didn't look at me. "I'm just following orders. Can I get or make you a drink?"

I noted the glass bottles of tonic water arrayed on the credenza and stepped beside Carmelo to take one. "Just this, thank you."

His eyes followed the bottle, then up my arm to meet my gaze. His lip twitched to a smirk. "Smart."

"What does that mean?"

Voices from down the hall stole his attention. Carmelo worked quickly to finish laying out his drinks and snacks. "I know you're busy, but based on what we were saying earlier, you should see the old fort ruins on the island's north end when you can. They're a fascinating bit of island history."

Wearing sunglasses, Eli pushed open the door for Andretti, then held it for Carmelo to wheel his cart out of the conference room and down the glass-lined hall. He craned his neck to watch the waiter leave.

"I am glad you're early, Mister Demetriou," said Andretti.

"And fully refreshed," Eli made an over-enthusiastic wink while snagging a tonic water from the table.

Andretti cursed, pulling my attention and saving me from thinking too hard about what Eli meant. The lawyer quickly cleared the ninth spot at the table, dumping the pretzels into the waste bin.

"Mister Romano, do better about keeping your work orders updated."

"I did that yesterday. I'll talk to him," said Eli.

"Problem?" I asked.

"A minor nothing," Andretti waved me off without looking at me as he pulled stacks of papers from his briefcase.

Eli sidled up to me. "Benedikt was supposed to be here." I could smell the rum on his breath.

"How well did you know him?"

He shrugged, his eyes a little glassy. "As well as you'd expect after a decade of playing cards with a guy twice a week."

"I'm sorry."

Eli patted a hand on my forearm. "Fair warning, Matty boy, I don't know how useful I'll be with how drunk and stoned I am."

He could have fooled me, but I couldn't see if his eyes were bloodshot behind his dark lenses. Maybe he swayed a bit more than one should, still holding onto my arm.

"Matteo, please," I said. "I haven't gone by Matty in years and would like to keep it that way."

"Understood."

"The others will be along any moment," said Andretti. "Mister Demetriou, I'd like you on this side, in the center, with myself and Signor Bianchi on either side. Mister Romano will sit beside Signor Bianchi."

"You got it all worked out, eh?" Eli flopped into his seat, swinging around to face the window and the sea beyond.

I heard more voices down the hall and hurried to my seat. It wasn't my imagination when Andretti watched me with unnecessary interest as I took a long drink from the bottle of tonic water.

"You and I are due another conversation after this," he whispered.

Giving up the video and list earlier had felt great, to divest myself of that intellectual burden. Now, I wanted to tell him all about Noah and my father's video. I was ready for that, to admit I'd still been holding out and promise to do better moving forward. "Fucking right," I replied, eyes on the glass in front of me.

Santiago led the group in some conversation, lost to murmurs through the wall. Giacomo strode like a mountain beside him, so much so that he would have obscured any detail of the general manager if he'd been the one walking closer to the glass. Vera Rossi followed by a few paces, her cream and white sundress flowing behind her. Her dark eyes found and locked onto mine immediately, piercing through me. Henrik Albrecht and Kenji Nakamura took up the rear. Henrik's lavender blazer looked like he'd just taken it out of a backpack, and he never looked up from his phone. He seemed oblivious to Kenji halfway hanging off his shoulder and stumbling along.

I made to rise to greet everyone as they entered, but Andretti stopped me with a firm hand on my shoulder.

"We are all here exactly on time," he said. "Allow me to introduce Rafael Demetriou's son, Matteo, the new owner of La Luce and Isola di Luce." He took his hand from my shoulder. It wasn't lost on me that Andretti introduced me as my father's son, but there were too many ways to read into that. It was essentially my only credential for being here.

My mother taught me manners, and that one should stand up to greet others, so I did. Santiago swung around the table to sit on my other side as the investors found their spots. Giacomo offered a hand across the table, and I took it, feeling like a child lost in his grip, large and powerful enough to palm a twenty-pound bowling ball.

"Unfortunately, we could not speak longer at the party yesterday. The music was too loud," he grumbled. "Shame about your old man, dropping right before the finish line."

I only nodded in response.

"My wife, Vera," he continued, waving at the slight woman in the Met Gala-appropriate dress to his side. She leaned an elbow on the conference table, drawing a nail across her lip as she considered me. My mother taught me never to offer my hand first to a lady, but wait for her. A raised eyebrow was all the greeting I got.

Wait... "Your wife?" I barely contained my shock.

Neither reacted, implying my response was typical. What a complex relationship the two must hav e... Or perhaps it was the simplest thing. A marriage for political and economic gain, but fuck whoever you please. I'd seen how Giacomo's trunk flopped as Carmelo railed him. Vera wouldn't survive that.

I shook away my thoughts. "A pleasure." Kenji had fallen into a chair with his head resting on the polished top and arms hanging loosely at his sides. "Is he okay?"

"He went hard last night," said Eli. "He'll be fine."

Kenji rolled his face toward me, drool running from the corner of his mouth. "Let me die," he groaned.

"He'll be fine," Eli repeated.

Rolling my eyes, I turned to the last of the four. "You must be Herr Albrecht. I'd love a closer look at your work on the water systems."

The engineer finally glanced up from his phone. He stared at me for a breath, confused, then like a light switch flipped in his brain, he grinned and slammed his phone on the table, screen down.

"Call me Henrik," he said in a thick German accent. "And anytime, just put it in my calendar. I wasn't aware you had a background in engineering and sustained fission reactions." His expression turned hopeful.

"I don't. I'm just interested in seeing what you've done."

"Ah." Henrik's shoulder slumped, and he leaned back in his chair.

"Let us begin," said Andretti.

Twenty-Four

Giacomo

ANDRETTI'S GAZE DRIFTED TO one of the vacant chairs. "I must address the empty seat. I am sure news has spread regarding Herr Jensen's demise two nights ago. The attending doctor has ruled it accidental, but we are still organizing the exact details. Until an official report is made, we ask everyone's cooperation in respect to his memory by quelching any rumors."

"Have you asked the son?" asked Giacomo.

"Or the lover?" asked Vera. I barely heard her breathy words across the table. That was definitely the other voice I'd heard outside the bathroom.

"Yes, the lover, the porter," said Giacomo.

Goddamn, did everyone know about Lio and the old tailor?

"Please," Andretti silenced them with a palm hovering over the table. "Trust that all inquiries are being made. Let us not add any unfounded suspicions to the pot."

Henrik snorted, snatched his phone to check the screen, and set it back down.

Andretti's gaze lingered on the engineer for a breath. "La Luce's grand opening has been on the books for two years, and I have brought you here today to ensure that everything is still on track. Mister Romano?"

Eli cleared his throat, far louder than was probably necessary, making sure all eyes turned to him. All eyes except for Kenji's. "The booze is here, the food is all ordered, and the DJ thrice confirmed."

"And the guest list vetted?" asked Giacomo.

Eli looked to Andretti, who nodded.

Giacomo laced his massive fingers on the table and leaned forward. "That leaves just two questions." He glanced at Vera, then focused fully on me. "What role will the new Mister Demetriou fill?"

Andretti cleared his throat. "Mister Demetriou has accepted his father's role of owner and CEO of La Luce."

"With what credentials?" Giacomo's eyes bore into me. "Five semesters at a liberal arts college and a CV overfilled with nothing jobs. He was a waiter, the attendant at a car wash, worked summers filling potholes on the freeway, before falling into a data entry position six years ago. Don't think I wouldn't do my research, Andretti." His eyes finally broke from mine, and I caught my breath before he focused on me again. "Nothing that speaks of what would it take to run La Luce. Then, his relationships, more than I care to enumerate, the longest lasting an inconsistent three years. Is this your lack of com-mitment or a deeper personal flaw?"

"Hey now, that's not fair," Eli said.

Giacomo held my gaze for another tense breath before his eyes flitted to Eli. "My wife and I have sunk a fortune into this island. Rafael Demetriou sold me his dream, but can this stand-in deliver?"

Santiago leaned forward. "Everything but the final touches is done. The mints are on the pillows, as it were. Mister Demetriou has some of the best, most dedicated staff I have seen in my long career. There is no need to question his credentials, not with the decades of experience at his disposal."

I felt the weight of everyone staring at me. Well, everyone except Henrik, who was back on his phone, and Kenji. I never liked being the center of attention, not from this many people at once.

"You ask what I might offer La Luce?" I cleared my throat. "I'm a fresh perspective, a new set of eyes. I'm decent with numbers and finding trends. I have a calm head and like to take the time to consider all angles of a problem. Yes, all my relationships have ended poorly, but they only lasted as long as they did because of my desire to help others. That can just as easily become a character flaw, but it's one I'm aware of and am working on. After doing my own research, I know I can offer La Luce one thing that none of you can, something that will be useful as the face of this resort..." I paused, licking my lips. "A clean legal record."

Eli snorted into his drink, Vera rolled her gorgeous eyes, Andretti sighed softly, and Giacomo turned a little redder.

"All useful traits, thank you, Matteo," said Santiago.

Giacomo's chest swelled, but Vera gently stroked a finger along her husband's forearm. He glanced at her, then at Andretti. "So everything is under control?" he asked, narrowing his eyes. "This man has assumed all of his father's contracts and debts?"

"Entirely," said Andretti. "Let us take a few moments to review the financial—"

"Question two," said Giacomo. "What about the shots fired on the island's north end two nights ago?"

That caught Henrik's attention, and he set his phone down, leaning back in his chair with fingers steepled. Eli and Santiago looked past me with poorly disguised surprise, awaiting the lawyer's response.

Andretti sighed and closed his financial report. "Locals were loitering, and security fired shots into the air to frighten them away."

"Is that so? The locals have been through enough and now they're being shot at." Giacomo folded his hands on his belly and leaned back. "A man's brains were dashed on the rocks two nights ago. Petras's people are shooting at locals the night before. Now Petras was suddenly fired this morning."

Eli snorted. "That was a long time coming."

Giacomo stared daggers at Eli, making him lean back in his chair before continuing. "Are we just getting all this violence out of our system now, before the opening? Maybe we should burn down more shops or throw someone off the lighthouse for good measure? That hasn't been done in a while."

"Enough," Andretti snapped. His hand was flat on his reports, but his fingertips curled, bunching the paper and ripping it from the binding. He didn't look up from where he stared at the middle of the table, but his face was beet-red. "Signor Barbieri, this meeting was an unnecessary formality. Your role is financier, and I will not have you question La Luce's operating decisions."

Giacomo pushed forward again. I could hear the bones crack in his fist as he slid into Andretti's direct line of sight. "That's where you're wrong. I was promised a return, and until I see it, I will question whatever I please and get involved as I choose. To that end," he glanced at his wife and back to Andretti. "In light of the sudden onslaught of failings, from security to leadership, we demand another ten points on our return."

"Impossible," Andretti said, knuckles turning white.

Vera hummed, freezing whatever Giacomo was sucking in a breath to say.

"I do not care for your story about shooting at locals, Mister Andretti," she said. "Does security lack proper training that they could not de-escalate the situation without resorting to guns? Would you like to add any detail?"

"I would not," Andretti said.

"And the fire?"

"An unfortunate, tragic accident. Mister Jensen is beset with grief," Andretti said, turning back to Giacomo. "Your returns are locked into your contracts. Any alterations at this point are impossible."

"Make it possible." Giacomo shoved to his feet, knocking his chair back. Vera rose smoothly beside him. He stormed out, and she quietly followed. It would have been more dramatic if they didn't have to exit the conference room and walk down the glass hallway outside it. When she was a step from leaving my view, Vera paused and glanced at me over her shoulder. Her eye twitched, and she was gone.

"I would buy out his interest, but I do enjoy his hotheaded drama," said Henrik. "So long as it is not directed toward me. What are your thoughts on establishing a board of directors, Mister Demetriou?"

"I would be for it," I said, glancing at Andretti to make sure he seemed to agree. He widened his eyes just a fraction, which I took as enough. "I would rather split ownership with shareholders than be beholden to return percentages written on bar napkins."

Andretti patted a hand on mine, chuckling. "That is quite an overstatement of the investors' relations to the resort, but your point is taken, Mister Demetriou."

Henrik glanced at his phone again and frowned. "I will take my leave. Thank you all, and nice to meet you, Matteo."

The four of us sat in silence on one side of the conference table for an awkward moment, broken by Kenji's quiet snores.

"I should get him to his room, then I have a thing," said Eli.

"Does the thing involve vodka?" Santiago asked.

"Always."

"I'll join you for one."

"Andretti, care to come with and tell us about this shootout?" Eli asked.

My phone buzzed, and I fished it out of my pocket.

"No, thank you," Andretti said while pushing the creases from his report's paper.

"Matteo? Vodka?"

I had a new message on the first ChatSphere thread.

+34 58 4115 7011: be careful

Careful of what? I was so sick of this person and their little warnings. But... who were they? I assumed at different times that it was Alec, Andretti, or one of the managers, but three of those four were standing around me. They'd gotten me the security footage, which surprised Andretti. Eli and Santiago were talking about getting drunk right now, not sending me messages. That left Agent Alec. Be careful about what?

I snapped back to attention with someone poking my shoulder. I looked up at Eli.

"No, but thank you," I said. "Raincheck, for sure. I also have a thing."

"Don't we all."

"He didn't mention the client list," I murmured to Andretti while stacking the papers beside him and watching the managers stroll down the glass hallway.

"I noticed, but doing so would reveal he knows more than he already should. Signor Barbieri still had his demands related to the security concerns. Commendable work defending yourself against him, though I worry you made an enemy despite any respect you may have earned."

"Thank you," I beamed.

"Go to your *thing*. Does it involve slinking?"

"It may."

"Mind your manners. I will clean up here." Andretti shooed me away from the papers.

I collected my paperwork, expressing a quick thanks as I did. That hadn't gone at all to plan. We were supposed to calmly discuss the water and power plant, finances, and party planning.

The route back to my suite was direct enough that I wasn't paying attention, focusing instead on the message and tapping out a reply.

+34 58 4115 7011: be careful

MinnGreekMatty: Of what?

Head down, I ran into a brick wall. Not exactly brick, but clad in expensive fabrics.

Giacomo grabbed a fist of my shirt's shoulder and dragged me into a breezeway between buildings, slamming me against the stucco wall.

"Now that we have a moment alone, I have a few questions for you," he said. His minty breath barely covered the smell of stale cigars. "Who are you working for? Really?"

"What? No one."

He ripped the phone from my hand and thumbed through my messages from the mystery number, eyes narrowing with his growing sneer. "Who is this?"

"I don't know, I swear." Fuck. Fuck fuck fuck.

Giacomo reached the top and snorted. "Well, they got something right."

"About my father?"

He shook me, popping my head against the wall. "I'm asking the questions. Were you hiding in the baths yesterday? What did you hear?"

"Nothing. I mean, nothing I could understand. I don't speak Italian."

He pulled me closer.

"We're supposed to believe Andretti found the fucking fabled Demetriou boy so close to the opening? You're working for the Markini Brothers." His fist twisted my shirt, pushing me into the wall.

Panic. Giacomo could crush me without effort. "I don't know who that is," I squeaked. "You listed off everything about my life ten minutes ago. You know who I am."

"Do not tell me what I know. Who then? Who are you working for?" He pulled back his fist, and I imagined him putting it through the back of my skull.

"That's quite enough," said a calmer voice. I dared look away from Giacomo to see Vera striding toward us. "Let him go."

Giacomo grunted and released me, giving one little shove for good measure. He stepped away as Vera took his place in front of me.

"My husband can get excited, but he means well." The cadence of her voice made me want to listen to her all day. No wonder she was an accomplished negotiator. "Your sudden appearance does raise questions, but if you ensure me that you are who you claim to be, we will believe you."

Her dark eyes locked on mine, and I had no choice; I couldn't look anywhere else. I might have believed she had magic powers from a fantasy tale, as the world fell away to include only those dark eyes.

"I'm Matteo Demetriou, son of Rafael and Sophia. I'm not working for anyone else."

She held that gaze on me for another heartbeat before blinking, and the spell was broken. "I believe you. It was a pleasure meeting you, Mister Demetriou," she said and stepped back, away from me. "Come, dear." She was halfway down the breezeway before I could breathe again.

Giacomo put a fist on my chest and leaned close, towering over me. "Maybe you didn't lie, but you work for me now, little man. Until I get my money, I own this place. Don't you fucking forget that, or I'll fuck you up. Or maybe I'll fuck you." He grabbed my wrist, pressing my hand against his crotch. I managed to wrench my hand from his grip as he followed his wife, laughing darkly. He tossed my phone over his shoulder after a few steps.

Adrenaline pounded in my temples, and sweat poured down my back. Four hundred pounds of muscle and rage wanted answers to questions I didn't understand. A man who could snap my neck with one hand or crush my head with both questioned my identity, and my only response was a weak retort that I am who I claim to be.

But who was I, really?

What did I bring to La Luce?

I was never anyone special until Marco Andretti rang the buzzer to be let into my apartment building. Even now, what had changed?

Watching my father's recording, I felt some urge to do my best here, but now it might be risking my life.

Fuck it.

I was going home.

Not home to the shitty apartment by the Taco Bell. No. I had millions in my private bank account. I could move to Spain. Or Norway. Find a hot Viking and snuggle under a heap of flannel blankets to stay warm through winter.

It was still mid-afternoon. I'd grab a few things from my suite, find a golf cart to drive to Xemxmarina, and get on the next boat or plane off the island.

My suite felt almost frigid after running across the resort. The elevator doors opened with a pleasant chime, and I rushed across the plush carpet, tossing essentials into an oversized gym bag. I'd left half my life in Minnesota, and now I'd only own what I could carry on my person. Stuff could be purchased again. I grabbed a few days' worth of clothes, my mother's gold cross necklace, and my writing journal, nearly full of chicken scratch.

I lingered in the mirrored hallway, staring at the closet with the computer. Did my father's video still exist on the hard drive, or had it self-deleted after I watched it once? Could I figure out how to copy it off somewhere? It was the only thing I had of him, saying he was proud of me, the only thing giving me pause from my flight. Maybe this was an overreaction.

The sound effect was from any dramatic movie or TV show, but it took a second to register, hearing it directly behind my head.

A pistol cocking.

Twenty-Five

Plea

"**D**ROP IT," THEY GROWLED behind me.

I had nothing to drop but kept my hands up, visible over my shoulders.

"Turn around, slowly."

I knew that voice, the out-of-place accent. With my hands held high, I turned in place so I had a pistol barrel pointed between my eyes, which was decidedly worse.

"Matteo." Alec breathed out his exasperation, and the gun twitched to the ceiling. He uncocked it and tucked it into the back of his shorts.

"Who else?" I let my hands drop, feeling anger flush my cheeks. He looked so annoyed after having a gun pointed at my head.

"It looked like someone was tossing the place," he waved at the clothes thrown across the bed.

"Well, it's just me." I shouldered past him. He fell back a step but didn't follow me back to the bed as I struggled to zip up the bag.

"Going somewhere?"

"Fucking right I am. I've had my life threatened twice in a half hour. I'm out of here."

"You can't leave."

"Fucking watch me."

Alec stepped beside me and put a hand over my gym bag. He exhaled close to my ear. "I need you, Matteo."

I turned to him, smelling his mix of coconut sunblock and a man who'd spent all day needing it. He was so close, hazel eyes pleading up at me, with his arm around my hip, hand still on my bag. Yesterday, I might have forgiven him for holding a gun to my head to know what his lips tasted like. The bed was mounded with the clothes I'd ripped through, but we had a couch and plenty of floor space.

No. This morning, sure, maybe. But enough had happened to ruin my libido.

I put my hands on Alec's shoulders. "No." I shoved him aside to get my toothbrush. When I turned, he stood in the bathroom doorway, blocking my path.

"Only you can save La Luce," he said.

"How's that? I'm the fable Demetriou boy that no one knew existed until Andretti went to fetch me. Fuck, I wouldn't believe I am who I am if I didn't see my similarities in the paintings of my father scattered around here. What special powers do I have?"

"I told you before, you're the only one without a laundry list of special interests here. You want what's best for the resort, which means removing the rot at the top."

"Wrong. I don't give a single tiny shit about La Luce or my father's legacy. At least not enough to die for it." I tried to slide past him, but he shifted to block me.

"You have to help me take Barbieri down."

I backed off, hands on my hips. "How did you even get in here?"

"The security is miserable. You know that."

Did he know the same trick as Lio, or was there yet another way to access my suite? Something else he said clicked, and I remembered Noah's pitiful whimper. I hadn't seen him, but I felt his terror with Giacomo looming over him, kicking him into the wall. "Yeah, Barbieri's a cunt, but what do you expect to do about him? His money's tied to La Luce. You can't take him out without sinking the resort."

A sly grin edged across Alec's lips. "A murderous crime boss funded this place, but your father was sneaky with the contracts. You have Barbieri's money and little more than a gentleman's agreement to pay him back."

"Sure. And if I don't, I'll be crab food."

"I have a plan for that. Where's the client list?"

I pushed past him, heading toward the kitchen. For him threatening to kill me a few minutes ago, I sure had no trouble pushing him around now. "I gave it to Andretti this morning."

"You what?" He stormed up behind me, slapping his hands on the kitchen island while I dug through cupboards for portable snacks.

"You're the one who told me to use it as I saw fit. I needed an ally here, and you've been MIA for a day and a half."

His hands clenched to fists. "How could you do that?" he screeched. "The risk my partner and I went through—"

"You don't have a partner, Alec. No one was shot. You just proved you can get in here when you want, so you probably printed the list in the first place. So tell me, why do you want to take down Giacomo Barbieri if you're working for him?"

"I'm..." Alec pounded a fist on the island and ran a hand through his hair, tugging his top knot loose. "He doesn't know it was me."

Fucking Christ, I was right; Alec was the hacker hired to get the list for Giacomo. "What does that mean?"

"He had Petras on the payroll and thought he was hiring someone in security, but I intercepted the message. We... have a history."

"Alec, I'm ready to skip out on all of this. I can't take everyone's lies and agendas."

"Do you want the long or short version?"

Why was I putting up with any of this? What could he say that would change my mind about leaving? Obviously something, or I'd be halfway to the village by now. "Short first."

Alec puffed out a breath and locked his eyes on mine. I'd been overwhelmed by his presence when we'd met on the beach. He'd been a big, strong man telling me not to get in his way but to do my civic duty for Interpol. Now I saw pleading in those eyes.

Though, he was still huge. "Two years ago, Barbieri drowned my partner in front of a dozen witnesses, including your father, and I want to see him brought to justice."

I could only blink for a few long breaths. "Maybe the slightly longer version."

"Could I have a glass of water?" he asked.

I grabbed a glass from the cupboard and turned the tap. It sputtered with air in the line but came to a steady flow within a few seconds. Watching it made me realize my own thirst, and I poured another for myself after sliding his across the island. I should be trying to find a route off the island, to start the rest of my life, not standing in my kitchen drinking water with an Interpol agent. Damn my curiosity.

He took a drink, and his shoulders deflated, relaxed. Agent Alec, the mysterious stranger turned terrifying ambusher, melted into something softer. I topped off my water and let him speak.

"I was assigned to an international crime unit seven years ago, at the same time as Skyler Reyes, who would become my partner. I touched a dozen cases involving Barbieri's network, but then I saw Isola di Luce in a file and the ties to La Luce. I'd always been intrigued by your father's case and the mystery of what he'd done to win this island. The paperwork is all there, all legitimate, but not the motives. Skyler and I were put on the team. We were sent here undercover, Barbieri discovered us, and held Skyler down in a hot tub while threatening everyone around that he'd do the same to them. I had no choice but to flee with the information I had. I never found out what happened to their body."

"Fucking hell..." I wasn't sure what more to say. He'd made up some tall tales already, but telling me about the gunfight on the north shore felt rehearsed in hindsight.

"Yeah... I doubt he'll ever see any justice."

"Even after what you collected over the years on him?"

"All circumstantial. He has armies of lawyers to sweep everything away." Alec rubbed a hand across his forehead. He finished his water, and I refilled him. "Not that the cameras work here, but there aren't any in the Turkish Baths, anyway."

My heart skipped. Giacomo murdered a person in... Where I'd watched him... Carmelo was clearly working for Giacomo. Had he been one of the alleged dozen? It was a wild story, impossible to believe, that Giacomo was so powerful that a dozen people wouldn't stop a murder. How many of them were Giacomo's goons holding my father and Alec down while making an example of Skyler? In my mind, Petras was there as well, though I couldn't decide whose side he would have been on.

Alec continued. "Taking down Barbieri, with all his vast network, will take as much as indicting a US president. He's paid off or threatened everyone to get to where he is."

"Then how?"

Alec pulled the gun from his waistband, set it on the marble, and spun it so the handle faced me. "As powerful as he seems, he's just an imposing figurehead. Remove his true power, and he'll collapse."

I stared at the gun. "True power..." I thought of the gentle touch on his forearm in the meeting, the calm words in the alley. "Not his power. His greatest weakness. Vera."

Alec nodded.

"What do you propose to do? Shoot her?"

"I'm not sure yet. I hate to say it, but I can't let you slip away yet. You're the only one with a background I can trust who can get close enough to them."

Thoughts of Giacomo's fist around my throat reminded me that I didn't want to be that close again.

"So," I let the word hang, taking another long drink. Having my life threatened was thirsty work. "You're clearly not here on official Interpol business."

Alec chuckled wryly. "Guilty. I'm using vacation time to avenge my—"

"Were you and Skyler more than just work partners?"

Alec nodded. "We did an undercover job as husband and spouse, staying in a romantic palazzo in Italy, and it ended up like a Hallmark movie. But with weeks of surveillance and meticulous note-taking. We couldn't be public about it, or they'd stop assigning us together."

"Not even justice, then. A vendetta."

He shrugged. "No matter my motives, know that Barbieri deserves what's coming to him."

"As long as it's not just a substantial return on his investment in an island resort." I refilled my water again. I'd been drinking a lot of tonic water over the last few days. Maybe this was my body's way of telling me it was dehydrating me. "Giacomo read through our ChatSphere thread, by the way. He seems to agree with you about my father being murdered."

His brow pinched. "What thread? I only sent you the one message."

Dammit, I'd been on a roll with my accusations. "Never mind."

"If you're working with someone else, I'd like to know, Matteo. You already gave up our only bargaining chip, giving the client list to the lawyer."

"That's useless now. Giacomo and Vera don't know where the list is and made a play for more money an hour ago."

Alec hummed his agreement. "It was a long shot. I needed something that would let me get near them." His eyes flicked to the gun resting between us. He leaned back, pinching his shirt to billow air down the front, then popping the top two buttons, giving me a preview of his barrel chest. Lio had a few inches in height, but Alec had at least another twenty pounds of muscle. A wave of dizziness washed over me, a sudden flush to the cheeks brought on by a quiet conversation between strangers regarding murder.

No. No one was getting murdered. At least no one *else* was getting murdered. Alec worked on Interpol cases regarding the island and my father for years. He could potentially provide the answers to so many questions I'd built up in the last days.

I glanced at the gym bag on my bed. If I left, if I was even able to leave, would I be able to live knowing what I'd left behind here? Besides the physical things Lio had carefully put away, what about answers regarding my absent father, who claims to have loved me? I would wonder about La Luce every time I withdrew from the bank accounts stuffed with its money. What was the origin of that wealth and would it ever come to haunt me later?

Alec rubbed a thumb along a silver ring on a chain around his neck, making me think of the ankh around mine. He bit his lower lip, eyes locked on mine as the silence between us stretched.

I reached forward, across the island. Something in his sheer vulnerability tugged at me, bidding me to comfort him, to hold him close.

I snapped back. No. What the hell was I doing and thinking? Alec was objectively great-looking, and vulnerability was a major turn-on, but I was always a one-guy-at-a-time guy. But... I didn't have a guy. Not Lio. Lio was a manslaughting, lying, violent, deceitful...

I cleared my throat. "You must know your way around my computer. Help me save off a file, and we can discuss what to do next."

His eyes widened. "So you'll help?"

"I didn't say that, just that we'd keep talking." It was as much an excuse to move so I would stop staring down his shirt. Andretti told me La Luce was to be an exclusive male-only resort, which I interpreted as an inhibition-free zone to fulfill all your male-only fantasies. It could as easily mean nothing about sex; just sitting around, drinking whiskey, smoking cigars, and discussing sports. I much preferred my interpretation and did not doubt the resort's success in it. If the climate or whatever was in the air could drive me wild so quickly, what would it do to the rest of the guests?

I logged in to the computer and pointed to the video file, relieved it was still sitting on the desktop. Alec came close, overwhelming me with his coconut sunscreen, and pushed me aside with his hip. He opened a drawer on the side of the station and fished around in its contents for a USB drive, which, thankfully or not, didn't match the one the surveillance videos had been stored on.

"I noticed this when I was in here the other night, but didn't want to mess with the encryption. What is it?"

The security message said several of my attempts had already been used, but that hadn't been him? "This is a video of my father talking to me. I don't have anything else of him."

He hummed, typing a few things into the side panel of scrolling green text, and shook his head. "The file's corrupted. Maybe something could recover it, but nothing that's installed on here. Still want a copy?"

Dad did say it could only be viewed once. "Sure."

Within a few clicks, he turned in place, handing me the drive. I realized I hadn't moved away when he'd worked his way to the station. I shifted to give us a few inches.

"Still leaving, Matteo?" Alec asked, crossing his hands behind his head, his elbows out wide.

I followed the flex of his bicep, up the veins popping along the muscle of his forearm, to his blond hair and how I'd like to run a hand through it. Maybe get a fistful of that top knot as I make him moan...

I shook my head and took another step back, but somehow didn't seem to get any farther from him.

"I don't know," I said, dropping the USB drive into my pocket. I leaned against the mirrors on the far side of the hall, as far from him as I could get, without feeling like I was fleeing. Swallowing hard, my vision swam for a heartbeat. I only wanted to close the space between us. Forget all the trauma of the last few hours with a few minutes of bliss. He adjusted himself with his free hand, giving me an excuse to look down at his tight shorts and the bulge growing toward his hip.

"For what it's worth," he said, pushing his hand in his pocket deep enough to expose the waistband of his underwear. "I apologize for pulling the gun on you. I didn't know it was you."

"That's okay. Thank you for defending my home." When had he moved closer? I was no longer leaning against the mirrored wall.

The distance collapsed to nothing. Our hands on each other's hips ground my cock against his. Foreheads pressed together gave me only a moment of shared breath space before his lips were on mine. My tongue explored his mouth. His hand slid down my back, under my clothes, to grip my bare ass. My mind screamed to stop while my hands worked at his cloth belt. I knew there were a hundred other things to do, a dozen lies to uncover, yet Alec leaned back his head with a soft moan as my fingers wrapped around his cock. He worked the rest of the buttons free of his shirt. He had one hand in my hair, pushing me down. I trailed my lips down his centerline while trying unsuccessfully to convince myself I didn't want to do this. My fingers wrapped around the waistband of his shorts and trunks, and there it was. Alec's cock was in my face. Perfect size, slight curve to the left, pubes trimmed, and balls tucked high with his arousal.

My vision tightened again. Had I been drugged? Alec too? We'd only had water in the last hour. That didn't matter. I needed his cock down my throat.

He gasped and clawed at the back of my shirt, pulling it over my head. My left hand was around the base of Alec's member, and my right shot down my front. Barely three strokes in, he dropped to a squat, pushing me back onto the carpet. My shorts were ripped around my ankles, and he spread my knees wide to kiss his way up my inner thigh.

I knew this was wrong. The little voice that nagged at me around Lio was now screaming. But that nagging voice came out as a gasp as he dragged his tongue up the right side of my ball sack.

"Alec..." I gripped a fist of his hair, holding him against on my cock. I pivoted my hips down and back up once, savoring how his tongue worked and how he whimpered.

He fell back, gasping, shorts tangled around his ankles. I felt it, too, like a twig snapping in the back of my mind. I scooted away and up to my palms.

"I don't know..." I sputtered.

"I couldn't stop," Alec said. "Like I was possessed."

I could only nod in response. Since arriving at La Luce two days ago, my libido had been on fire. This felt like a concentrated dose of that. If we hadn't pulled ourselves apart, we wouldn't have left a single surface of my suite clean.

"What the fuck?" I breathed, watching my hands shake.

Alec stood, pulling his shorts with him, giving me just a second to steal one more look at what I didn't take the time to appreciate a moment ago: thick thighs, a muscled core with a realistic amount of body fat, and hair across his chest leading a trail downward.

"Something in the air? A super-sonic signal broadcast through the wiring? The water?" He offered a hand down to me.

I refused it, standing and shifting away another foot as I did. His eyes flicked down my naked body briefly, then he made a show of averting his gaze. He'd tossed my clothes down the hall after tearing them off.

"La Luce is intended to be a place without inhibitions, but that was more. I didn't feel in control of myself," he said. "Not that I hated it. It just wasn't what I was planning on doing."

I stepped into my linen pants, wishing I could shower first, to take a moment to wash away the stress and sweat and... and whatever just happened between us. "Same," I said. "On both accounts."

Without looking back and my shirt hanging from my fist, I left the mirrored hallway for my bed and the packed bag.

Alec followed. "What do you say, Matteo? What just happened was as much reason to stay as leave. What are you going to do?"

I had the money to fuck my way across Europe or buy a secluded castle in the Scottish Highlands, never to see another person. Either would leave me forever wondering what had just happened. That wasn't something I could let go.

Turning to him, I nodded. "I'm staying."

He grinned. "Great. Do we need to talk more about what just happened? Do we need a safe word for the next time we start having sex?"

I knew he was joking, but the feeling of not being in control of my body, of feeling like a helpless passenger in the car, had been terrifying. It had happened so fast and was over just as quickly.

"We'll see," I said, forcing a grin.

He pinched the point of my chin between his thumb and forefinger, winking.

Twenty-Six

Nap

AND SO, I DECIDED I'd stay. I had to know more. What happened to my father? How did he acquire the island? Why did I want to fuck everyone on the island? Well, that was an easy answer. The real question is, what about the island that made it so I couldn't stop myself? I'd had my life threatened before. What openly gay man living in America hadn't? The mortal threat had never been quite like seeing Giacomo's fist pulled back or feeling the cold steel of Alec's gun against my forehead, but those somehow felt less. They threatened me because of what they thought I was doing, not because of who I am.

Alec rushed out, saying he had an idea he wanted to follow up on but wouldn't tell me more. I told him secrets don't make friends, which I thought we were trying to be, but he still refused to say anything. I understood it as him not actually having an idea, just wanting a reason to get away and process what had happened.

I changed into my swimsuit, thinking Enzo might approve of it, but his father definitely would not. Lined with compression spandex rather than uncomfortable netting, the dark purple shorts were spotted with bright blue crabs. Yeah, I'd be whimsical. With my earbuds pushed in and a paperback book in hand, I left the ankh necklace on the nightstand and made for the infamous pool under my balcony. The pool that Alec stood beside, watching me, and where I'd found the USB drive yesterday.

I wouldn't be alone. Two men about my age lounged on the far side of the water under a dark blue umbrella. One rolled on his side as they conversed and sipped from half-empty fishbowls. I recognized them from the mixer yesterday, but not enough to remember their names. Eli had told me the two were new money, winning the jackpot in a multi-state lottery. My takeaway was that La Luce wasn't just for those with political or social clout. They just needed lots of money. A third man swam a lazy lap, and it took a moment to recognize it was Kenji swimming in a tiny black Speedo. He'd apparently recovered from his hangover. The one on his side raised his glass in greeting, triggering the other to turn and wave. I returned it but moved to the chair farthest from them. Were I any closer, whatever force had overpowered Alec and me might have me asking about making space for a fourth under that umbrella. Not that I'd be against that, but... professionalism...

Laying out in the full sun, I knew the paperback book wasn't going to happen in the glare. I wouldn't be practicing my language lessons in public, so su-doku it would be. Not even that held my attention long while I considered the last two days. The client list would hang over Andretti unless I told him the rest of what I knew about Alec, but that might just go away on its own. Herr Jensen wasn't murdered. I didn't think Lio was aware of the will's change, which might also clear itself up. One nagging detail revolved around my father, but he'd died a year ago, so it clearly wasn't urgent. I'd have to do some-thing about Giacomo and Vera. How does one prove they're not working for a competing crime ring? Did they really just want the client list to get more money from me, or was there a deeper plot?

"Would you like your umbrella adjusted, *sinjur*?" someone asked in a soft voice. Long sleeve pink shirt, light blue pants, undercut.

I shaded my eyes up at him. "Carmelo?"

"How was the meeting?" he asked, opening the umbrella nearest me. Probably not a bad idea. I hadn't put on sunblock.

"Eventful, though not productive."

He went to a silver cart with a refrigerated cooler a few paces away and returned, offering me a cold, lime-infused tonic water. "You should make sure you stay hydrated in the sun."

I watched the slow bubbles rise along the inside of the clear plastic. "Why did you insist on tonic water yesterday?"

"The tap tastes a little off, don't you agree? I'll be right back."

He wheeled his cart to the patrons on the pool's other side as Kenji pulled himself from the water. Even without hearing anything they said, I could read it in their body language. The three men laughed a little too easily, freely touching each other while keeping their eyes on Carmelo. The waiter gave it right back, playing with his hair, smirking, and running his hand across Kenji's wet chest. If I'd been over there, I would fully believe this cute waiter had a genuine interest in me—a skinny waiter in tight pants outlining the bulge running halfway to his knee. I watched him pour three shots of some clear liquor from a small bottle, but they insisted on a fourth. They tapped glasses, knocked back their drinks, and all but Carmelo coughed and choked on it. They recovered slowly, waving down his questions about needing anything else, raising their existing drinks, and taking sips as a chaser.

I kept watching them as Carmelo wheeled back toward me. Kenji made a gesture along his inner thigh, and the others had clearly noticed it as well, waving their arms to estimate length and girth.

"They look like they're having fun," I said when he stopped next to me. I opened the tonic water while he mixed me a drink. Hopefully, an Old Fashioned.

"They are. I look forward to the guests like them, who just want to have a bit of fun without making a fuss." He stirred in a few drops of simple syrup, measuring nothing. "The taller one lying closest to us, Benj, asked me to give him a tour of the lighthouse. I wonder if that's all he meant."

"Cheeky. I suppose most of the guests will treat you like that."

"I have fun, they have fun, and they tip," he winked.

"What was the name of your village?"

"*Baħar Antik*," he said. "Ancient Sea. You can still see bits of it around La Luce. A wall here, a converted church. If you have a chance to see the Turkish Baths, the building is completely original to my village, though the inside was altered." He stared at me while stirring the drink, the single ice cube clinking against the glass.

There was something too direct about it. Why mention that particular spa a day after what I'd seen happen in there? Giacomo ordered him to get close to me, but the man was clearly unstable. Maybe Carmelo was fishing for what I knew. Maybe I could give Carmelo a hand.

"I'd love to see it. What else would you recommend of the island's history?"

"The old fort ruins at the north end, I think I mentioned that, along with the lighthouse. They're particularly breathtaking around sunset. Bring water. It can be a long hike."

It kept coming back to the lighthouse. "Henrik offered a tour of the water and energy plant up there, but maybe you could show me around more intimately?"

"Sure thing," he winked, handing me the glass. "You have my number."

Did I? I guess I could get ahold of any of the staff through some directory I hadn't looked for yet. Plus,

Carmelo had to live on the island somewhere. Wait, that was something else I'd never asked.

"Where do you live? I didn't notice staff housing on the maps, but I suppose they wouldn't label that for guests."

"Thinking of paying me a visit?"

I chuckled, "That's not why I asked, not quite."

"My apartment is on the west edge of Xemxmarina. I have a private balcony overlooking the bluffs. Very private. I could tell you all about the island's history, and no one would hear us."

I swallowed hard.

"Pardon me, but duty calls. I like your crabs." He wheeled away, returning to the trio, waving for his attention.

His statement perplexed me for a beat until I looked down at my trunks and their little blue crabs.

I'd never been the target of such aggressive flirting, but I liked it. Back in Minnesota, guys wanted me, but because I had a decent job or because I was marginally darker skinned than the rest and had curly hair or because I was that rare uncircumcised unicorn. Carmelo and Lio showed interest for their own reasons, but at least they wanted to take advantage of me for reasons I hadn't experienced before.

Carmelo poured the thruple another shot, doing one himself after plenty of animated attempts to decline. There was more laughter and more casual touching that lasted a few seconds longer than required. Carmelo handed one of them something, maybe a business card, and wheeled away while the three stared at it, clearly unsure of what to do next.

They decided quickly, gathering up their discarded things and leaving in the direction Carmelo had gone. I couldn't take my eyes off them, giggling and chattering to each other. I tasted copper and realized I'd been biting my lower lip. The Old Fashioned, crafted to perfection, did nothing to wash away the taste. The taste... of jealousy? Anger? Was I actually upset at these three guys that they might be about to do something that involved Carmelo being naked? That was absolutely none of my business.

As much as I tried to convince myself it was irrational, I still felt my face flush and heart pounding down to my fingertips.

Maybe this was too much time in the sun and heat. I finished the tonic water, letting the tart sweetness calm the heat down my throat. Leaving the bottle and unfinished cocktail on a tiny table, I took my untouched book and returned to my room.

My suite's AC washed over me, clearing my mind. What's a little bit of heat stroke, especially when caught early? My crab shorts didn't make it four steps into the room before I tossed them toward the couches. The bed called to me, sang to me, even. It had been a long trip and a whirlwind couple of days, uprooting everything about my life in the last week. I fell onto it, crawling toward the pillow, but didn't reach it.

A chime woke me, and despite the fog in my brain, I recognized it as the elevator call alarm. I rolled over, ignoring it, but it sounded again.

Falling out of bed, I managed to land on my feet and shuffle to the elevator. Lio grinned up at the camera, holding a ribbon-wrapped box with "Dolce Mare" stamped across it. I could ignore it and pretend I wasn't in, but he might use the override and come up anyway to drop off his package. I noted the time at the bottom of the screen, almost six. I'd been asleep for over two hours. Three inconspicuous bars sat in the bottom right corner of the screen, which I tapped to reveal a list of selections along the right as the image of Lio darkened: Custom Greeting, Access Log, Privacy Mode, Lockdown, Settings. I tapped Access Log, and a gallery of snapshots replaced smiling Lio. There was a fish-eyed shot of me coming back from the pool, going to the pool, and all my comings and going in reverse order. There was Alec as he left after holding the gun to my head. Lio in just his blue shorts after his manslaughter of Herr Jensen and beside it fumbling for the armholes in his pink top. Scrolling further, I saw Alec leaving with the client list and shortly before when he entered. Lio and Alec's images had an extra icon in the top corner, of two arrows chasing each other in a circle.

Why was there any question about the client list with this? Andretti must not have known about it. Great, my father kept secrets as well.

Before that, the timestamps were weeks apart, showing staff with cleaning carts, wearing a handyman's belt, or a few with Andretti. Then... The man himself, Rafael Demetriou, often intermixed with the lawyer and less so with dozens of other faces. The earliest date was over two years ago.

I dismissed it all to the image of Lio looking a little impatient. I tapped to accept him and went to find a pair of shorts.

The doors dinged a few seconds later.

"Mister Matteo, I brought you— Oh." His eyes ran over me as I pulled up the loose shorts, then he focused on my hair with a grin. "It's not often a sexy naked man answers the door for me." His gray eyes flashed wide with a devilish grin, and he set the wrapped box on the low table beside the bowls for keys and change. He prowled toward me, raising a hand to run fingers through my hair, but I dodged him. "What's wrong?" he asked.

"Lio, you have to leave."

"Why..." He glanced back at the package he'd brought up. "I thought we could get sushi, then finish what we didn't last night." He stepped forward with an arm extended, meaning to snag my waist, but I slipped away with a dining chair between us.

"This is happening too fast. I keep telling you that, but we keep ending up together."

"Doesn't that mean it might be fate?"

"It's been two days, Lio! Something's not right on this island. Don't you ever feel like you're not in control of yourself here?" I glanced down the mirrored hallway.

He opened his mouth to say something but let it hang, his eyes growing distant as he no doubt rethought his last two years.

He rode me an hour after watching his ex-lover die, and I didn't stop him. The very thought turned me on then—a memory that would go down as one of my darkest. After what happened in the hallway with Alec, I knew I hadn't been in the right mind since I landed on the island. Was Lio aware of my impairment and taking advantage of it?

No. I saw it in the emotions warring across his eyes, how his brow crinkled and jaw tensed. He was innocent, at least relatively so. Lio had withheld from me, but I'd done the same to Andretti. I circled the chair to take his hand. "Lio, what we did two nights ago after Benedikt... That can't be us."

"What are we, then?" he asked, not meeting my eyes.

"There's a lot going on, not least of which was you hitting Enzo." I raised my hand before he could interject. "No matter what he said or did, violence should never be the response. I think the best thing for everyone right now would be for you to stay at home. Until things are settled, we have a working relationship and nothing more."

Lio's right hand curled into a fist and relaxed just as slowly. He turned and slapped the elevator call button, which opened immediately. "It would explain a lot if there's something in the air here. Now I'm not sure if anything I felt for Benedikt was real."

Benedikt left millions to Lio; the tailor obviously thought he felt something. Would he have admitted that to Lio in the zen garden if Enzo hadn't shown up when he did?

"All that aside, I just want to kiss you, Mister Matteo." He stepped into the elevator, adding, "Keep the donuts," as the doors closed to his back.

That actually hurt... There couldn't be anything real after such a short period...

I heard a thud and rushed to the control screen, tapping it to show Lio leaning his forehead against the elevator car's mirrored wall. His shoulders heaved with heavy breath, arms hanging at his sides. I watched until the doors opened, Lio straightened, rolled back his shoulders, and exited.

I scrolled through the settings for chime style and volumes to find one called Access Override with the same icon beside it as the one Lio and Alec's gallery images all shared, which I turned off. Then, Reset Key Access, which asked for a confirmation before informing me it had cleared all other access codes and asked me to wave a key over the sensor at the bottom to reprogram.

Finally, Lockdown bordered the screen with diagonal red slashes.

I stepped away and blew out a breath, finally feeling secure for the first time since Andretti told me about the client list over drinks. My eyes landed on the box of donuts, but I denied the pang of guilt that tried to creep in. I only wanted Lio for what I hoped he was—a tender, thoughtful man who wanted to care for me—but I could see what he actually was—a violent, manipulative liar just looking to attach himself to the next guy to take care of him.

Though the encounter was brief, I felt the start of a migraine as I came down from the spike in blood pressure. I'd already napped longer than intended, but I deserved just a little more. Kicking off my shorts on the way back to bed, I was asleep within minutes.

My phone chimed from the nightstand, ruining the most restful sleep I'd had yet on the island. Cobwebs dragged away the feeling of whatever dream that left me hard. I ignored it, with some difficulty, more out of spite. The windows were dark. So much for a one-hour nap.

My stomach grumbled. When had I eaten today? I'm sure I could still order something. Or find something in the kitchen. Or Lio had brought donuts.

The phone chimed again.

Straining, I managed to get my fingertips on it where it sat on the edge of the nightstand without moving too much. 9:43pm. Another four hours gone. But so what? I needed the sleep, and nothing else was on my calendar for the day. Then I saw the notification. That damned blue globe. ChatSphere. Of course it was fucking ChatSphere. Two separate threads from unknown numbers. The string of chats nagged at me. Why was one a chain of messages from the first I'd gotten two days ago, but the other a single message I couldn't reply to? I guess I assumed there was some error combining the chat thread, but what if it was more? Were there two or more senders? I tapped into the new, solo message.

Unknown: 911!!

Then, the second.

Unknown: come to water treatment
plant, found something huge -Alec

At least he signed it this time.

The obvious revelation crashed down on me, stealing my breath for a moment.

"You have my number," Carmelo had said. I'd been right. The string of messages was from someone who had been at dinner that first night but not sitting at the table.

Twenty-Seven

Water

I SQUINTED AT THE message. Somehow, it being signed by Alec made me doubt its authenticity. I imagined Alec tied to a chair. Giacomo holding a gun on him and Vera leafing through his phone.

I swiped to the other thread, reading through the messages with renewed clarity. Carmelo was working for Giacomo Barbieri in some capacity but feeding me information, maybe hoping I could stop him, like Alec hoped I could. Carmelo told me to go to the Turkish Baths and warned me to be careful after leaving the investor meeting, a warning I had ignored. I don't know how he'd gotten the security footage.

Giacomo said a bit to Noah before I turned on my translation app. What if Noah worked in security and gave the USB drive to Carmelo, who was also at the mixer, who then snuck it to me afterward? What if, what if. I loved my sudoku and other brain teasers, but I developed more theoretical mind games in the last two days than I had over the last year.

Throwing on something that smelled clean enough, I grabbed a tonic water and called for the elevator.

The water treatment plant sat on the north end of the island, where most interesting things seemed to happen: shootouts in the bluffs, suicides at the lighthouse. It was not an easy walk, but that was certainly by design. Anything loud or industrial should be kept well away from guests. By some divine grace, a golf cart waited for me outside the lobby with the keys dangling from the ignition. I slammed on the gas, the electric engine buzzed to life, and I careened out of the tiny lot at eleven miles an hour. The cup holder gave me an opportunity to unscrew and slam half the tonic water. I hadn't drunk anything in hours and was sweating out more than I was taking in. I didn't notice the bitter bite as much this time, drinking it quickly, but the cool aftertaste was refreshing.

I flicked my eyes up to keep on the road lit by the half moon and the cart's headlights as I left the resort's grand and beautiful buildings and shifted close to a row of olive trees. I pulled out my phone, thumbing through to call the only contact I had on the island outside of ChatSphere.

It went to voicemail on the second ring.

"You have reached the voicemail of Marco Andretti. At the tone, please leave your name—"

I hung up. Who actually recorded their message? I swapped to send a text.

Me: water treatment plant, come at once

Ahead, a gate was thrown wide in the chainlink fence. "No Trespassing" signs in a dozen languages dotted it. Around another curve of olive trees, the ruined battlements of a limestone fort came into view. Its walls were seamlessly patched with new construction and modern-looking double doors.

Carmelo told me twice to visit the old fort, which housed the water treatment and energy plant. How had I been so dense to think they'd be completely different structures? I followed the battlements west to where they ended in a lighthouse that doubled as a guard tower.

Another cart, much nicer than I was driving, was parked beside the entrance. I had never considered luxury electric carts before, but this was one. If Hummer made golf carts, this would be it. From the wide tires to the reinforced chassis, everything looked rugged with just a little extra girth. Had Alec stolen that to get here? Unless... who would want such a custom cart?

Four hundred pounds of Italian muscle and anger might.

Fuck.

Fuck fuck fuck.

The wide area in front of the fort might have once been used for military drills when the French held the island, but it now served as a parking lot. I was pretty sure it could house all the vehicles on the island, and I parked at the farthest spot. A smaller door blended into the fort's side, and I jogged across the gravel to it. Why would Alec call me here if Giacomo were around? He wanted to take down the bear, but a bit of warning would have been nice. With a hand on the door's level handle, I paused, again imaging Alec tied up, his phone in Vera's cool grasp, and spittle flying from Giacomo as he demanded to know more about the Markini or Scoleri or whoever other brothers while pressing a gun into Alec's temple. They had known he was behind the client list, but their reasoning had to be more than getting another five or ten points on their return.

My heartbeat drowned out the distant churn of water as I tugged the handle.

Locked. The keycard pad beside the door taunted me with a tiny red light. The walls ran to the cliffs and a sixty-foot drop to the rocks, leaving only the front entrance beside the industrial-grade golf cart.

I checked my phone for a response, but Andretti might as likely be inside the plant with the investors. Maybe Henrik was in there, too, giving them all a tour. I crept toward the front door, realized that was ridiculous, and jogged to it, pausing again. What was my plan here? Was it even possible to form a plan knowing nothing about the situation within?

Inhibitions, hesitation, and plans be damned. I yanked the door open, entering the wide lobby. Informational posters covered the walls describing the revolutionary desalination and purification process used in the plant. Colorful diagrams broke down the basic details of the fission power system integrated here, showing how it outperformed a dozen other types of energy production. All were topped with the ReinKraft logo, resembling an atomic model with whizzing electrons, except the nucleus was a green and blue planet Earth. This had to be Henrik's company, or at least the division of it present on the island. Weird it wasn't mentioned in the dossiers. Future guests might convene in this space for tours. A line of white hard hats hung on a wall beside another door leading further into the facility with another taunting keyboard beside it. Except this one glowed green.

Cleanliness washed over me when I opened the door. Cool, damp air hit me, and as deeply as I breathed it in, it was never enough. Whatever had been within the fort for five hundred years had been scooped out for criss-crossing metal walkways spiraling down to a swirling vortex sixty feet below.

Andretti mentioned it as an off-hand remark when we first arrived that the need for freshwater was something my father had solved early on. This was the true genius that would lead to La Luce's prosperity: net positive power. Henrik's machine drew from the Mediterranean Sea and turned it into potable water and energy, creating more than it took to run. La Luce, and the whole of Isola di Luce, had an infinite surplus resource to trade. All the spas, Michelin-star restaurants, pristine beaches, and sexy staff in tight uniforms came second to this. The gravity of what this ancient fort held never occurred to me until I stood within it, hands on the catwalk's metal railing, looking sixty feet down to the churning waters. The stairs and metal walkways spiraled downward at the building's outer edges. Each of the six levels ended in a room and continued to the next, making the structure a giant hexagon. Pipes lined the walls, but everything led to the swirling vortex of water at the bottom. I squinted into it, imagining I could see a tiny spark of pure white deep below the surface.

From my high vantage point, I caught movement on the walkways below and saw Giacomo down a few levels, flanked by Vera. They appeared to be in casual conversation with no guns or hostages in sight. She glanced my way, and I shot back against the wall. Unless she knew where to look, she couldn't have seen me in that instant, I hoped. I counted to ten and dropped to a squat, barely peeking over the rail, and saw they were gone.

Alec was somewhere in here, hopefully not on the other side of Giacomo and Vera.

I tried replying to his ChatSphere message but got an immediate undeliverable message.

I wasn't a man of action any more than I was a detective, yet I moved to the stairs, making my way to the next level.

The roar of water below grew with every step down the first level as I aimed for the room at the end of the catwalk. Dials showing unknowable metrics lined the wall below a wide window overlooking the water. I kept moving, creeping down the stairs, vigilant for any sign of Giacomo and Vera. My heart sank as I stepped into the next room, fearing Alec's message didn't mean entering the plant, and he was waiting outside for me.

A hand clapped over my mouth, dragging me with irresistible strength into the shadows.

"Shh!" a familiar voice hissed into my ear and flipped me to face him.

"Alec, what the fuck is going on?"

"There's something in the water." He was still gripping my shoulders. His eyes were bloodshot over dark bags. He'd clearly been going nonstop since leaving my suite. "They're putting it in there."

"Giacomo and Vera? What are they adding?"

"I don't know. I don't know who's involved or who knows what, but it makes you do things you wouldn't normally do. Some powerful drug that interacts with the fission reactor."

I tried to pull from his hold. "You're hurting me."

Alec released me, staring at his hands as if they'd acted on their own.

I couldn't take another mystery without clearing out the last. "Are you actually Interpol, or did you get that badge from Party City?" I rubbed my aching shoulder.

He blinked, frowning. "I am, or was. I was discharged a year ago."

"You're just here for vengeance, not trying to bring Giacomo to justice. Do you have any proof they've added something to the water?"

Alec ran a hand through his hair and retied his top knot. "Nothing concrete, but it makes complete sense. I bet the sink in your kitchen hasn't been used in a year. Remember it sputtering when you poured us a drink? Whatever Barbieri added was sitting in the pipes, becoming concentrated. That's why we..." He mimed his fists slapping together.

Carmelo's insistence on tonic water, saying the tap tasted off. The waiter was too sly for me.

"Barbieri deserves to die, Matteo," Alec said.

"He's funding the resort. Even if we've already cashed the checks, he's bursting with powerful contacts. Do you think you'll shoot him, and everything will be better?" I waved at the gun tucked into the front of his shorts.

"I better make it a good shot." Alec pulled out the gun, unloaded the magazine, and showed it to me as if I knew what that meant. He must have noticed my confusion. "I only have two bullets."

Rarely had I so badly wanted to hit another person in the face. I'd never survive a real fight against Alec, but I wanted to throw the first punch right now. I settled for shoving him, but he barely moved. "You broke into my suite, printed highly confidential information that puts the whole resort at risk, then gave it back to gain my trust. You have to hear how stupid that sounds."

"You'd be surprised. Almost the same thing worked in Rio nine years ago. We don't have time for this, Matteo."

"Don't have time for what?" asked the familiar, gravelly voice, followed by the too-familiar click of a pistol.

Twenty-Eight

Power

G IACOMO BARBIERI FILLED THE doorway leading deeper into the plant. The gun in his fist looked like a child's toy, but I had no doubt it held more bullets than Agent Alec's.

Before a few hours ago, I didn't have experience with what to do when a gun was pointed at me, but I did the same as when Alec threatened me. My hands shot up, and I took a step from the agent.

"*Sapevo che non potevamo fidarci di lui,*" Giacomo grumbled, waving the pistol and urging Alec and me closer to the window.

"Don't be rude, dearest," Vera purred as she stepped around her mountain of a husband. "You know his Italian is weak."

"Why should I be punished for that?" Giacomo growled.

Vera placed a finger on his forearm, lowering his gun arm, and turned to Alec. "You owe us something. Is that why you are here?"

I watched the ex-agent in profile, his eyes narrowing, smooth jaw tensing. Vera wasn't fibbing. Alec said they didn't know it had been him they hired, but she knew.

"I don't know what you imagine accomplishing, Agent Alec. You were paid for a service, and that service lacks only delivery. Give me the client list, and you may walk away."

I had to do something to split Giacomo's attention. "You've been working for them the whole time?" I slid farther from Alec, and Giacomo raised his gun in response. "I'm guessing your sob story about wanting vengeance for your partner was all a lie, then?"

Alec squeezed his eyes tight, shaking his head.

"You're still going on about that? That was years ago. Get over it. I have." Giacomo snorted, then laughed, throwing his head back to let out a single guffaw.

As quick as Billy the Kid, Agent Alec pulled the gun from his waistband and fired. The shot's deafening roar echoed through the small control room.

Alec rolled back his shoulders and leveled the gun at Giacomo. "This ends here, Barbieri."

"*Figlio di puttana—*" Giacomo clapped a hand over the crimson stain spreading under his left collarbone. He coughed once, spattering blood before him, and raised his gun again. The bear rushed forward, firing again and again, slamming into Alec and knocking them both back and through the doorway toward the catwalk. Alec flinched and staggered with the shots, but it all happened so quickly, I couldn't tell if and where he'd been hit as Giacomo slammed them through the door.

"Alec!"

I rushed after them onto the catwalk. Giacomo pinned Alec against the railing, dented at his lower back by their impact. Giacomo roared something in Italian, bloody spittle flying, and smashed his fist across Alec's jaw. He pulled back for another hit, and I rushed forward, as if I had a chance of stopping the grizzly.

A single, soft-spoken word cut through the din of the water and the pounding of my heart, freezing me.

"Halt."

Vera stood in the doorway, Alec's gun in her hand, pointed at me.

Giacomo grunted a choking, wet laugh and railed once more against Alec. The agent's jaw and cheek had to be broken, maybe the orbital bone, too. He could barely open his right eye to look up at me, pleading, blood pouring from his lips.

Pulling back his fist once more, Giacomo embedded it deep into Alec's gut, bending him forward. Then, with the same motion, he lifted Alec, shoving him forward and over the railing. The force almost took the grizzly as well as he caught himself and lost sight of Alec in the roiling vortex below us.

"Good work, dear," said Vera. "That takes care of one loose end."

Giacomo laughed, leaning hard against the railing and pressing a hand to his chest wound. He gasped something in Italian about needing a doctor.

I finally wrestled my focus from where Alec had gone into the water, seeing red when I looked up at Giacomo's bloody smile. "You motherfu—" I only made a single step in my rush toward the bear when the gunshot rang out behind me. Giacomo raised confused fingers to the blood gushing from his throat, and he toppled backward.

I looked over the railing a heartbeat later; the image searing into my mind of Giacomo Barbieri lying on a tangle of pipes. His twisted limbs bobbed awkwardly as the current tried to yank him into the vortex.

"And there is another loose end. How tidy things are becoming," said Vera, stepping beside me, tossing the gun into the water. "Two men with an old grudge finally ended each other. We, two people of slight build, could do nothing to pull them apart."

I looked up at her, suddenly towering over me. "Your husband..." I sputtered.

She drew a derringer from her tiny handbag I hadn't noticed before, and I shied backward, hands raised. Her eyes lost some of their focus, but her expression didn't change as she looked down at her husband's mangled corpse.

"Giacomo was good to me for years, and I will miss the companionship and security he provided, but that's all there was between us," she said. "Now that he's gone, it falls to me to consolidate our assets. I see a lot of consolidation in my future, especially with the rivals who wanted him dead."

"The Markini Brothers?"

"Good memory, Mister Demetriou."

I surprised even myself, remembering the name Giacomo spat in my face as he threatened me in the alley. "Were you really interested in getting more on your investment, or was this all an elaborate means of killing your husband?"

"Can't it be two things? Are you trying to stall?"

"I'm sure I'm more valuable alive."

She rolled her gorgeous dark eyes. "That may be so. You've tidied another thread by firing Petras. I paid Alec to get in and steal the list and paid Petras to create a path for him. They came up with the story of the shoot-out here on their own. It was an idiotic plan, which I told him would only serve to give Mister Andretti an ulcer, but my husband could never keep well enough alone, always picking what was otherwise fine. Now we're free of all that. If Petras comes forward, his story will sound like the raving of a disgruntled ex-employee. The agent's body will soon be floating in the Mediterranean, never to be recovered, and I will play the widow in black. That leaves only one loose thread, Mister Demetriou: you." She tightened her grip on the gun.

"What about the client list? I know where it is."

The gun dropped an inch. "You are skilled at stalling. I don't care about the list anymore. The climate is too hot to move forward with what we intended."

"Why is the list so important? It's a list of sixty-some men. You can't sell that to a newspaper."

There was the eye-rolling again. "You are a simple man. If you were throwing a party, would you not like the guest list in advance? Would you not want to be able to cater to every whim and desire?"`

It dawned on me. The client list was useless to the outside, as something less than tabloid fodder. But to someone who could prepare and design the most damaging situation for each guest... Vera and Giacomo were planning what I'd fantasized about but on a much larger scale. "You were going to blackmail everyone."

Vera nodded. "Maybe not completely simple." She waved her gun for me to approach the dented, blood-smeared railing. I couldn't stop myself from stealing another glance at Giacomo thirty feet below.

"They struggled, locked in their one-sided grudge," Vera whispered, barely audible over the water. "They fought against the railing, and the ex-agent went over. My dear husband reached for him, hoping to save the man who wanted him dead, but he tipped over the edge as well." She focused on me. "Valiant Mister Demetriou rushed to save him but slipped, and they all went over." Her grip tightened. "These damned slippery catwalks. I hear a Spaniard went over just before my husband and I arrived."

"Noah," I gasped. I was napping while Noah was kneeling on this catwalk, begging for his life with Giacomo's gun against his skull. Could I have saved him had I taken more action? My desire to keep a few secrets to myself might have led to his death.

Vera's eyes widened a hair. "You are a well-informed little thing, aren't you? It's almost a shame you have to die. Almost."

"What did you put in the water, Vera?"

"It's just a little something that mixes well with Albrecht's machinery, helping to loosen the belts, lips, and wallets of La Luce's clientele. It's nothing you need to take to your grave, Mister Demetriou."

The waters churned and frothed far below, greedily awaiting the moment I'd join them. Would it be better that I land in a broken heap like Giacomo so my corpse could be recovered? Or be washed out to sea like Alec, Noah, and my father? "We can work this out," I said, barely controlling the shake in my voice. "We can work together."

"You're a terrible actor, Mister Demetriou," she scoffed. "I offer you a choice. Let yourself over the railing or force me to shoot you several times in very painful and embarrassing places. I assure you, I can summon the strength to lift you over once you're done struggling."

I could rush her. I'd seen a Western documentary years ago that said the guns, like the caliber of the one in her hand, were not often deadly, at least not in a single shot. How many shots could she get off in the time it took me to close the ten feet between us? If she landed a fatal hit, maybe I could take her with me, knocking her over the railing to meet the same fate as her husband and Alec.

Where was Andretti? I should have texted him again or called before coming down here. I shouldn't have come down alone. That was about to cost me my life.

"Could you tell me something, Vera? Final request?"

She sighed but twirled her gun.

"Your husband pointed out my string of failed relationships, and it's true. I thought I was in love a few times, but I never was. My life is a string of failures and squandered moments. You make it sound like you and Giacomo had a marriage of financial and political alliances, but you had to have built up love over the years."

"There must be a point or question amongst all your ramblings."

Did I have a point beyond delaying her for a few breaths? "What did that feel like, to love someone?"

She had to know I was stalling before she killed me, but how often would she get the chance to consider such a question again?

"Love is the sum of all the little things that a person does that show they care for you, or you them," she said. "Does that answer your question?"

Like leaving someone breakfast in the fridge. "Maybe, but what about—"

The shot rang in my ears, and pain blossomed in my foot. I looked down more in surprise than anything else at blood soaking through and welling up across my shoe.

"No more talking," said Vera. "Jump and be quick, or I'll make this slow."

I'd experienced my share of pain. Broken bones, a torn ACL, but this was different. My mind disconnected, like my body told it there was an injury, but my brain was too confused and overwhelmed to accept it, didn't know how to process it beyond that first stab of the bullet. All I knew was I didn't want her to shoot me more, but I didn't want to take her first option, either.

I sprang at her, aiming my shoulder at her stomach, hoping to bowl her over and down. But my foot slipped in my blood, and she was too nimble for me, easily sidestepping. I fell on my chest and forearms beside her, bashing my nose against the catwalk's grating. I stared through to the swirl below while tears welled up in my eyes, as much from the broken nose as the circumstance.

Vera's knee pressed against my spine, and her little gun into the back of my skull, pushing my head down and against the grating. At this range, I'd be dead, no matter the caliber. "I've changed my mind, Mister Demetriou." Her words tickled my ear. "Tell me where the client list is, and I'll make this quick for you."

"Why? You said you can't use it."

She gripped my hair, painfully pulling my head away from the grating. "I don't need it but its existence is a liability. I want you to die with nothing."

I could tell her it was in my front right pocket. I'd roll over to get it, kick her knees or face, whatever was convenient. The fight would continue. I might win.

Instead, I squeezed my eyes tight. "Fuck you, bitch."

There, barely visible through my tears, half hanging at the catwalk's edge just out of reach, Giacomo's gun.

"I had hoped to rein you like we did your father. Violence was always my husband's department, not mine, but I'll make an exception for you." She took her knee off me to stand, and I quickly rolled to my back, throwing out a fist to catch whatever of her I could.

I completely missed her, but kept rolling to lunge for the gun, tipping it over the edge in my haste. As it fell, the shot behind me blasted over the water's churn. I felt nothing. Maybe this was what it was to be dead, and I didn't know it yet. Except... the rush of water returned to my ears, and my foot still screamed at me. I looked back, seeing Vera just as confused as she toppled toward me, and I raised my arms to deflect her weight to my side. Crimson spread across the front of her dress while her lifeless eyes stared at me.

Marco Andretti knelt at the doorway with a gun leveled in both hands. He slipped it into an inner breast pocket as he stood, eyes flicking to the streak of blood on the rail. "Is this what slinking looks like, Mister Demetriou?"

Twenty-Nine
Lighthouse

WHY DID SHE HAVE to shoot my right foot? It really only mattered when driving, so it mattered now as I pulled up to the lighthouse just before sunset, three days after I was last in this parking lot.

It could be dangerous out here on the north bluffs at night, with the uneven ground leading up to the old lighthouse. A wrong step could turn an ankle and send you to the rocks below. I tried not to glance back to the modern entrance along the limestone wall leading into the water treatment plant. I tried not to think about what had become of Alec and Noah as I scaled to the old wooden door. It swung gently, unlatched. Someone else was inside.

Within, the last rays of the day shone through the few cracks in the outer walls and reflected down from the lamp room. A spiral staircase with a rickety wood rail followed the curve to the room above.

A shadow shifted up there.

I sighed upward. Eighty-five steps with a booted cast. This would be fun.

Winded and sweating, I reached the top and sat beside the other occupant with feet through the safety railing ringing the lamp.

"What now?" I asked.

Marco Andretti never turned in my direction, eyes unfocused toward the horizon.

"Four dead in three days," he sighed. "Yet we must go on."

"Five," I corrected him.

Andretti hummed his agreement. No one had witnessed Noah's death, but neither could anyone find him. The lawyer had first fought me, saying the IT agent would be considered a missing person, that he might have stowed away on the same boat as Petras, but he knew better.

One hundred and fifty feet of air separated us from the rocks below. If others were to be believed, my father jumped or was pushed from his spot. It would have taken three seconds for him to hit. Just enough time to realize what was about to happen. Maybe enough time to regret having done it. I bet that three seconds felt like an eternity.

"The seed of doubt you wedged into my mind has taken root," said Andretti.

"Meaning?"

"The doctors all agreed that your father's symptoms pointed to ALS, but always with a hint of suspicion, I realize in hindsight. Their next breath always asked for tests or samples, which Rafael refused. I have started wondering if your father was aware of a poisoning plot."

"And killed himself? That doesn't make sense."

"No, it does not."

Andretti didn't want to believe in Noah's demise because there were no witnesses or a body, yet he had no problems imagining my father tossing himself to the waves. "What about the water? Do we know it's safe to drink?" I'd told Andretti about every encounter, as much as it made me blush while he swirled a glass of red wine in his office two days ago. He dismissed my worries until I arrived at the interaction with Alec, where we both felt a complete loss of control.

He shook his head. "Herr Albrecht has yet to find any hints of sabotage in his plant. The trace molecule he discovered in the water has been found in every source, but there is no origin yet. The samples sent to laboratories in Italy, Greece, and Spain have yet to identify it. They have confirmed alcohol and acid quickly break it down, as well as extreme heat. We cannot delay the opening because of this. We will ply the guests with booze and tonic water to neutralize it."

"I don't know how I feel about drinking unknown molecules, even if the bourbon will render them inert. What about the mister fans outside half the doors?"

"We have almost two weeks to solve it and devise the correct ratios of additives to make the water safe."

"Knowingly drug the clients while not knowing the source of the problem, gotcha. And three of the five key investors are dead, yet we're still moving forward?"

"Yes. I know it sounds cold, it is cold, but we have their money. As dark as it sounds, some may wish to come if only to tour where the dreaded Giacomo Barbieri died."

I winced, not entirely sure if he meant it as a joke. "Let's not lean into that on the marketing posters." The lawyer had killed a person in my defense three days ago, and though we'd talked about a number of things, we hadn't brought that up yet.

We watched the sky darken in silence with the sun setting to our backs.

"I found a video on my computer from my father."

Andretti leaned his head against the rail and looked at me, waiting for me to continue.

"He, ah, said how he regretted leaving me and Ma in New York, never bringing us here."

"That would have been difficult, as well as dangerous. Your father dealt with more than one persona similar to Signor Giacomo Barbieri."

"Why did he get involved with crimelords? Henrik and Kenji seem like great guys. Why get money from people like Giacomo and Vera?"

"Herr Albrecht and Mister Nakamura only signed onto the resort once it was in motion. Why build a bleeding edge power station with no one on the island to need power? Why fund the parties where there is nowhere to party and no one to party with? We needed a great deal of quick cash to get started, and that never comes legally." He sighed. "I take it you got into the video file. I must ask you, what was your father's only regret?"

"You... You were the other failed attempts?"

He nodded. "I knew it existed but never knew the contents. I sought you out only after failing to open it."

"Matty," I said. "I was his only regret. I assume he regretted abandoning me, not my existence."

"It was the first. He talked about you often in our private moments. He believed in what we were creating but wished you could be involved. Curious, I tried your pet name as the password. M-A-T-I?"

"M-A-T-T-Y."

Andretti hummed and nodded once. "That would have been my next guess, but I didn't want to risk losing the file."

"He said Petras' blackmail isn't valid anymore, though I don't know what it was."

"Curious again. Petras claimed he was in possession of incriminating documents regarding overt crimes that resulted in Rafael acquiring the island. I fail to see how that is no longer valid. I put a man on him, to watch where he scurries off to after being ushered off the island."

"Maybe there was more that my father didn't tell you."

"That is unlikely." Andretti's unfocused gaze toward the horizon made his meaning crystal clear. He'd come close to admitting it directly in his office, that he and my father were lovers when he said men of his generation weren't allowed to say that. I'd act surprised if he ever felt comfortable enough to tell me.

I sucked a breath in through my teeth. "Well..."

"What?"

I told him about the archival footage on the elevator clearly showing Alec using the override to enter my suite and print the list. I didn't tell him about the few I found of him and my father entering the elevator together, all business until the doors closed. Then they dropped their briefcases and... I quickly closed those. Andretti's shoulders slumped as he listened, otherwise impassive. I hated to be the one to tell him the man he loved was withholding so much, but he had to know.

"I put a man on the porter, as well," said Andretti. I tried not to read into it as something vindictive. *I can't trust my man, so neither can you yours.* "He is still in his apartment in Xemxmarina. If Mister Jensen chooses not to press charges, he is free to leave or return to work. We can hardly hold a manslaughter trial for the grand opening."

My phone chirped, and I pulled it from my pocket. Carmelo hadn't been at work in the three days since everything at the water plant, but at least he finally replied to my ChatSphere message.

> MinnGreekMatty: You okay?

> +34 58 4115 7011: Keeping my head down, I think I caught something.

> MinnGreekMatty: Stay safe. I look forward to an Old Fashioned on that balcony.

> +34 58 4115 7011: Soon, I'll let you know.

"Anything I should know about?" Andretti asked, watching me thumb my response.

Why was I still withholding from the lawyer? I'd told him everything that had happened since landing but carefully scrubbed Carmelo's presence. Maybe it gave me the illusion of agency, to know I could keep all the secrets I wished, but that illusion might have added to Noah's death. Over the last few days, I learned how much I needed Andretti and that I should trust him. However, telling him now about Carmelo would spoil a great deal of the goodwill built between us. I was already in the middle of telling him about a message I'd kept from him for days. I'd find another time to weave in Carmelo.

"It's nothing," I said when I realized Andretti was staring at me.

He sighed. "As for Herr Jensen's will, I have yet to find an avenue of attack. Not that I have had an abundance of leisure time in the last few days. We may be welcoming the porter back as an investor to sit between Herr Albrecht and Mister Nakamura. We cannot legally withhold this from him much longer."

If Lio were an investor, or at least independent and not reliant on a job at La Luce for his well-being, would that change anything between us? If he found out and still wanted to run my bath... I wasn't sure what to think, knowing I'd been drugged while we were together. I at least had my share of tonic water and liquor to fight what Vera put in the water, but Lio didn't drink.

"Anything else?" Andretti finally asked.

"My father said he left another message for you, leaving it in your special place."

Andretti jerked back from the railing at that, eyes wide. He pushed to his feet, nearly running into the lamp room. I followed him as quickly as I could with my injured foot. A small bookshelf, only hip-high, sat next to a threadbare couch. Andretti tossed the moldering books over his shoulder until one caught his interest. Turning to me, he dropped the book but held a business card in his other hand.

"What's that?" I limped toward him.

He turned it toward me, but the characters were Greek and meant nothing.

"The Den of Dionysus," he said, flipping the card again and tracing a thumb along its edge. "It's just outside Larissa, Greece. It's where we first met. Where we first started to dream about what would become La Luce."

I stood beside him, looking over the discarded, rotting books piled on the floor and the pristine business card. "What does it mean? He said he left a message."

"He did." Andretti brought the business card to his lips. "He wants me to follow him."

THE END

Also By Dirk

Other works by Dirk Mourningwood
La Luce's Legacy (2024)
Eros Unzipped (2024)
Eros Unchained (2024)

About Dirk

Dirk Mourningwood is an emerging voice in the world of MM erotica, known for his bold storytelling and captivating characters. With a passion for exploring the depths of human desire and the complexities of male relationships, Dirk weaves tales that are both sensual and emotionally resonant. His writing invites readers into a world where passion knows no bounds and love transcends all barriers. When he's not crafting his next tantalizing story, Dirk enjoys immersing himself in period dramas, practicing kenjutsu, and playing disc golf with his lab, Rodger.